BIRD IN THE SNOW

For Cathy

BIRD
IN THE
SNOW
MICHAEL
HARDING

THE LILLIPUT PRESS
DUBLIN

First published 2008 by
THE LILLIPUT PRESS
62–63 Sitric Road, Arbour Hill
Dublin 7, Ireland
www.lilliputpress.ie

ISBN 978 1 84351 136 6

3 5 7 9 10 8 6 4 2

The author acknowledges the assistance of the
Arts Council of Ireland and Centre Culturel
Irlandais, Paris, during the writing of this book.

A CIP record for this title is available
from The British Library.

Set in 11.5 pt on 15.3 pt Hoefler by Marsha Swan
Printed in England by Athenaeum Press Ltd, Tyne and Wear

BIRD IN THE SNOW

GUSSIE

I

SNOW IS FALLING like tufts of cotton. Snow beyond measure. Covering the mountains and touching the sky. Falling through the bushes and weighing down the trees. The mountains white and the lakes frozen over. And Birdie, standing in her pale-blue dressing gown and her red tattered slippers, as the snow spirals around her in grainy flecks, like the cosmos coming into existence.

She crumbles the bread as quickly as she can. And before long there are two little robins and a wagtail and three fat blackbirds around her feet. Landing and taking off. Hovering and diving and strutting around her red slippers in the snow. It's panic stations. The snow is covering the bread as fast as she drops the crumbs. And eventually the little robin, who knows her well, who knows her like a mother in winter, comes and lands on her fingers as she works a crust. And his bravery earns him great rewards. For he can pick enormous chunks from the feast in her hand as he perches on her thumb.

She loves her birds. The grip of their tiny claws on her fingers. The breath of wind as the wings flutter near her cheeks. The peck of a beak on the back of her hand. The cawing and twittering in her ears.

It's a long time since she had first felt the tickle of their feathers on her nose. That was in Dublin, just outside the train station. She was a little girl. Her father was beside her; they had come up for the day. And as she stepped down onto the platform, she saw dozens of white pigeons making a feathery halo around the silver head of an old lady who was standing in the middle of the platform, her two arms outstretched like Christ on Easter morning blessing the world. A poor old woman, wearing a man's black coat and laced boots, and smiling a toothless smile at the astonished child.

The old lady asked her if she would like to give the birds some bread, and Birdie pleaded with her father, and her father agreed to a limited experiment. He was a whiskered man from east Galway.

And that was the first time Birdie squealed with delight as the birds landed on her arms and fingers, and dug their tiny claws into her skin. Now she's over eighty and herself an old woman.

But she can't delay in the garden. No, she must get back to the house immediately. Not just because the snow is seeping into her bones with alarming speed, but also because today it is her lonely duty to attend the burial of her only son.

There's always talk at a wake. Everybody gossips about what the corpse looks like and what he died of. Everybody is sorry. And everybody says, what if ... As if somewhere in the dark folds of the universe there might be other possibilities. A parallel world where things happen differently.

What if Gussie had stayed at the teaching? Maybe all this might never have happened. What if he had married

8

the long, lanky girl he was doing a line with years ago when he got his first job. What was her name? Louise. That's right. Louise. And how many years is it since Louise walked out on him? She dropped him like a hot potato. The mourners could talk the hind legs off a donkey. And Louise had lovely legs. Twenty years later, everyone still remembered her legs. They were like a horse's hinds. They were towers of ivory. And she had long, blonde hair down to her waist.

If only he had signed himself into the hospital earlier. If only he hadn't signed himself in at all. People seem to love dead bodies, tragedies and smelly things in the wardrobe or under the floorboards. And then they'd say, sure, it's all for the best. And it could have been worse, they said. He didn't die in pain. He didn't know what was happening. And thank God it's all over.

On they went for hours, as the corpse lay far away in a cold chapel, and Birdie wished she could go out under the dark night sky and dig the grave herself, and throw him into the watery hole of starlight. Just to get it over with. She would tumble her own little baby into the black earth with her own bare hands.

So many people came to shake hands with her. The teachers who worked alongside him for years arrived. The nurses who knew him in the hospital appeared. Father Lee, who kept an eye on him when he went missing, slithered in. Even Louise flew across the ocean. And Birdie was glad to see her standing at the front door, after all those years.

For fifteen years, Gussie suffered from an irritable bowel as they call it now. He taught in St Angela's Secondary School in Kinnegad and lived in a flat in Mullingar, which deteriorated over the years. The central heating broke down. The curtains fell from the windows. The floor sagged and squeaked. And the toilet was what Birdie described as the Black Hole of Calcutta.

But it was the irritable bowel that held Gussie in a state of emotional paralysis. He lost his only girlfriend before he was twenty-five, and remained frozen in a timeless bubble of sorrow for the next fifteen years. Birdie didn't know why. At first she thought there would be a cure. An end. A point where surgery or tablets would rectify everything and he would return to the person he once was. He would take up life again. But he didn't. Nothing changed from year to year. And eventually she accepted that nothing was ever going to change. And she would never really know who her son was.

The irritable bowel can be a hard taskmaster. He never had any comfort. In the supermarket or the post office, or maybe at a filling station, or buying oranges at the news-agents, it was all the same. Even on the few occasions that he went for a walk in the flat countryside of east Galway, or on the plains of Westmeath, where there were neither hills nor ditches for the unfortunate man to hide his shivering bottom. Birdie pitied him. Crowded spaces brought him out in a cold sweat. The classroom wasn't too bad because he was always able to dash down the corridor to the staff-room, though there was no telling what states of hysterical laughter those young girls reached, on such occasions.

Parent–teacher meetings were a disaster. They were a ritual humiliation. Squirming in front of the local court clerk, Trevor Higgins, with his neat, black moustache, and black wool coat, and his trousers creased like razor blades. Higgins, a posh little peasant with a good job, who spent his summers in the south of France and got his clean, white underpants in a twist of rage and irritation when he had to confront Mr Mediocrity, as he described Gussie.

Gussie never made much progress at teaching Alicia Higgins her irregular verbs. And it was all dragged up at the parent–teacher meetings. Alicia was lanky and as tall as himself, and she was all blushes and shy in front of Daddy, as if butter itself wouldn't melt in her mouth. As Daddy began tearing strips off the teacher for his inadequacy in the French tongue, Gussie would go beetroot and invariably fart like an officer's horse, so that eventually Alicia would come close to wetting herself in the effort it took to avoid laughing.

Then there was the school principal, Mr Crosby. He was some tulip. And down on Gussie like a ton of bricks when he got the chance. He used to play rugby. Not blessed with a sense of humour. Enormous lips the colour and texture of dough, which were always squeezed into a zero as tight as a duck's hole when he was displeased with a student's behaviour. That was his nickname. Duck's-arse. Didn't Birdie have to listen to her son whingeing one night that Duck's-arse was always picking on him? And what do you mean picking on you, his mother wanted to know. Sure you're not a student. Aren't you supposed to be one of the teachers?

Crosby's face was flat. Something like a lump of dough that someone had fisted. His nose was broken and had never been fixed right. His ears were chewed to their stumps. If you met him in a bar, with a pint of beer and his head shaved to the roots of his follicles, you'd be hard got to figure out was he a policeman or a criminal. But anyone would guess that he was one or the other.

It was certainly difficult to think of him as principal of St Angela's Secondary School, on the outskirts of Kinnegad.

He could barely squeeze himself in between his glass-topped desk and his black plastic swivel chair. Such weight!

Gussie cringed for fear the seat would collapse.

Then Crosby stared at his keys. He had a lot of keys. Forty or more dangling from a large steel ring. He was like a prison officer. His head lowered. His big fat paws on the keys. On the desk. Tapping with his sausage fingers.

'I'm a little concerned about some of your days off last year, Mr Delaney.'

'It's a medical condition, Mr Crosby.'

'Arah for fuck's sake, I know that Gussie. For Jaysus sake, I know. You tell me that every fucken year for as long as I've known you. The question is ... have you ever seen a doctor?'

'No.'

Gussie often practised holding on. Tensing up his face muscles. His jaws clenched and his teeth hurting his eyeballs. His legs starting to shiver, as he tried to hold the muscles of his arse closed against that sudden quake and mighty force of his own personal waste. He stopped the car at every turn of the road and did it up against wooden gates that opened on to fields of barley and sugar beet in the middle of nowhere. He evacuated behind ditches of bramble and in forests of spruce trees, in rain and wind, in summer heatwaves, and in the middle of the night at the roadside, with the headlamps of passing cars blinding his eyeballs.

You're lucky you weren't arrested, Birdie said to him once. If anyone saw you doing that, they'd probably phone the police.

He even managed it one time in the car park of Dunnes Stores in Roscommon.

'Ah Gussie. Could you not go into a bar or a hotel or somewhere? Did you not notice that you were in the middle of the town?'

Then there was the food. That didn't help. About once

a year she would chastise him about the debris lying around his flat in Mullingar. The old cardboard containers for frozen pizzas and the tins of processed rice scattered on the work-top. The empty snack boxes from the local chipper stuffed in plastic bags under the sink. There was no end to it.

'You need a maid,' she said. 'And you need to eat vegeta-bles,' she told him. 'This place is disgusting.' He gazed at her in confusion and without comprehension. He was like a beast lost in a fog of solitude, not knowing where the cliff was any more. She often saw that look in him and there was no denying it. He was bewildered. She knew he'd be swal-lowed up eventually. The fog of his own confusion would win and he'd go off some deep end, like a calf wandering over the side of a mountain.

Birdie is in the kitchen. It's the middle of the night. She's boiling the kettle. She's thinking about everything. Birdie didn't come down the river on a bicycle. Nor was she born yesterday. And though she always saw the sun and moon shining on the ground where her son walked, there were some odd moments, as the years went by, when her unconditional love could not mask an unbearable revul-sion. Especially when she heard about the trouble with the schoolgirl. That was the kind of incident that Birdie could not gloss over. It was not a good sign.

Loitering. No other word for it. Loitering around teen-agers. In the quiet corner of a chip shop in Kinnegad, skulking for hours like an unwanted dog, at his age. And he would gaze at all the pretty little schoolgirls, munching their dinners, as his hands trembled on the tabletop. His ears so finely tuned that he could move them with the flexi-bility of a rabbit as he eavesdropped on their girlie gossip. His breath no louder than the whisper of a sleeping cat, and his heart pounding in his ribcage like a stag in the forest of love. To be so close!

And then one day there was just a single little doe-eyed student sitting there, with freckles and long, sandy hair entwined in a single pleat, and dressed in the neat green uniform of the school where he taught. And she was crying at the table in the far corner. Gussie opened the *Daily Mirror* in front of his face and then stole a sly peep over the top. Her head had already crashed into the bottles of vinegar and the red plastic container of tomato sauce. There was no one else in the shop. So he went over to her. He always looked like a goose that had gone round the wrong corner in life. Didn't Birdie often say that to herself?

And in the chip shop the little cherub was trembling, as if some invisible devil had wrenched the tears one by one from her breast with a long hot tongs. Yet despite that distress, she couldn't but notice the teacher staring into her eyes as if he had seen a fairy dance at the bottom of a well. Her French teacher standing above her, open-mouthed and drooling. That's what she saw. Or so she said. That's what the schoolgirl said. Drool.

And gossip travels faster than electricity. I hear your boy is in trouble with the school, her neighbours bleated, when Birdie met them in the church porch. Little women full of mock compassion. The parish as vigilant as a cobra's eyeball. The streets whispering, Tut tut!

But he was lucky. For weeks the school authorities negotiated with the parents' solicitors. Birdie never quite got to the bottom of a recurring phrase in the legal correspondence: 'disputed facts'. She heard Gussie's version. That sounded innocent enough. But what part of the child's anatomy did he touch, as he towered over her?

Birdie never knew. Whatever the young girl claimed about her encounter in that desolate chip shop, it never reached Birdie's ears. The parents agreed that an apology from the teacher would settle the matter without further recourse to the law. And that was the end of it. Although in a way it was only the beginning.

2

BIRDIE SITS UP in bed. She's still awake. She has joined the legion of sleepless old mothers who sit up for hours in armchairs and sofas, on pillowed bed-rests and on toilet seats, in the middle of the night. Mothers staring into the black night at the end of it all, and all of them thinking the same terrible thoughts. Birdie had sacrificed everything for him. She had done her very best to rear him properly. And then when he went out into the world, as broken as a bird with a dead wing, she crucified herself wondering where she had gone wrong.

Sometimes in his childhood years there were long periods when she couldn't even touch him. If he was upset from arguments in the schoolyard, or lonely because his playmates had gone off fishing without him, she would always tell him to go upstairs and have a bath. That was his little treat. The bathroom was a menagerie of plastic shampoo bottles and bubble bath in the shapes of Donald Duck and Mickey Mouse, and his bedroom was chock-full of teddies, and furry creatures from every cartoon under the sun because she thought that giving him teddies to hug was the same as hugging him herself.

Now look at her. Sitting up in bed. Struggling to find the light switch. Gawking at photographs in the big leather-bound album. Her little boy smiling out at her from the bathtub, his head all lathered with soap.

Oh he was a great child for the bath. And afterwards he would stand on the rug, dripping wet, his bum to the open fire, and a towel tied around his skinny waist, at the hips. She would chastise him playfully for not putting on his pyjamas, and later she'd come in with a smaller towel to dry his hair, and there were moments in that ritual that felt like hugs, when faltering laughter rippled from both of them and seemed like a faint intimacy. But that was before the electric hairdryer came into the house. The hairdryer spoiled everything.

When he was at college doing his Arts degree, he missed his baths, and he never mastered the craft of washing in those tiny, plastic shower units that were fashionable in apartments of the seventies, with green plastic curtains that clung to his legs like cold fish, and made him shiver, and hoses of water that were either too hot or too cold, and had as little pressure as an old man pissing.

Even while teaching in Kinnegad, he insisted on renting a flat in Mullingar, a larger town forty minutes up the road, because he wanted a spacious bathroom. He was so happy with his Mullingar flat that he often stood in front of the electric heater, naked, playing an old, black penny whistle that had survived since his childhood. He didn't drink. He didn't smoke. He never went out. So maybe it was harmless enough to sit in front of the television for almost two decades. That's what she told herself. She was his mother for goodness sake. She wasn't going to construe anything nasty about her broken boy. But the incident in the chipper was a turning point. There was no happiness after that.

The following summer he brought up the subject of Cornagore; he announced his intention to go back there, for a holiday. Birdie nearly went through the roof. Cornagore, in Connemara? On his own? That godforsaken windswept bog! After all that happened there in the past! Was he right in the head? Don't answer that!

Anyway, he went. And he went alone because, as he told her, he needed some space.

Some what? Some space. Some solitude, says he. Some privacy. Birdie didn't see it like that. It's not solitude he needed. The last thing in the world he needed was more solitude. Wasn't that what was wrong with him? Indulging himself in far too much solitude for fifteen years and stuck inside that fucken flat in Mullingar.

But private space is what he got. Buckets of it! Because Cornagore, in the far end of Connemara, may have been a holiday resort, but it was nothing remotely like the holiday resorts advertised on television, with brown young girls in G-strings sauntering along golden beaches. There were very few brown naked bodies outside Cornagore, where he booked himself into a bed and breakfast. And not a G-string or a bikini in sight. Just barbed wire and fence posts. And cows grazing in the sand dunes. That's the brown naked bodies that were waiting for him. And him a teacher that could have passed the entire summer in Benidorm or Majorca with all the other teachers. All summer long if he so wanted, in his shorts, with pina coladas and ice creams, at bamboo beach bars. Isn't that where he should have gone? To the Costa del Sex.

Birdie might look a bit strange, sitting up in her big-pillowed bed in the middle of the night, but she's no daw.

She's not an ostrich. And what young people do now is nothing different from what they did fifty years ago. Or one hundred years ago. Just because she's old, people think she doesn't know what young people do on the beach when they've had a few drinks. But Birdie knows. The question is did her poor gobdaw of a child know! Or maybe he knew too much? And maybe he saw too much too soon.

Off he went to Connemara, on his own, and though the beach was empty and windswept, he still combed it with a shrill and desperate longing, from morning until nightfall. He walked the long, white strand each day with the stride of a military man alert for enemy ships, his coat flapping in the wind. He continued through June and July. He phoned home a few times but all either of them could say was hello. And then they'd both listen to the crackle of the line and the silence sizzling all the way to Mars and back. She knew that wasn't good.

He paced that beach like a man demented by atrocities. Like his insides were full of car crashes or burning buildings or mining disasters. Unspoken fatalities. Hidden slaughter. Up and down the beach, as lonely as a cormorant left behind in a storm, and if there were any girls lurking in the region, or within an ass's roar of that blighted beach, then they certainly made every effort to avoid the long lanky drip of misery in the black coat who paced the shoreline like the ghost of a ship destroyed.

The landlady phoned Birdie at the end of July. She was a young woman with a husky, seductive voice, the soft precise vowels of an uneducated country girl, and a lifelong devotion to Our Lady of Lourdes, and she felt obliged to tell Birdie the truth. And when Gussie was still sitting at the breakfast table in her bright, floral bungalow, two weeks after the phone call, on the Feast of the Assumption, she told him it was time he paid his bill and went away. She just couldn't bear it any longer.

'Eight weeks is a long time to be anywhere,' she said, wiping up cornflakes and spilled milk with her jay cloth. Her that wasn't anywhere else in her life, except for two weeks' honeymoon when she was nineteen. In the Canary Islands. And not a nappy or a cot to be seen in her clean little guesthouse five years later. Birdie knew the type. Thousands of babies lost inside her and no permission to mourn, or scream. Just light candles to the Mother of God and keep the house spotless.

'I mean, what if he had an accident or something? I wouldn't be able for it.'

A nice way of putting it but Birdie knew what she meant. She meant that if she went into his bedroom one morning and found her floral bedspread stained burgundy red with ten pints of Gussie's lifeblood, then all the rosaries and novenas she had said in a lifetime wouldn't protect her from losing her mind with rage. Young woman. Married at nineteen. Two weeks in Tenerife. Doesn't that say it all?

'A long time to be anywhere,' says she, and she hadn't been out of her little Laura Ashley house in a lifetime. Rosaries and novenas and videos of the pope to keep her tranquilized. Birdie knew the track. You don't live as long as Birdie without learning something about human nature and the religious imperative.

'He's very odd,' she said at last on the phone to Birdie. It was like a thump in the face. An accusation. A full stop. It stopped Birdie in her tracks.

'Are ye there, Mrs Delaney? Are you still on the line? I hope I haven't said anything to upset ye.'

'He is odd,' Birdie admitted. 'He is.' She was crying. 'And I'm sorry.' And she hung up.

The days shortened. The sky filled with cloud so heavy and low that it felt as if slabs of cement were pressing down on the earth. The phone didn't ring again. No more dispatches from Connemara. And Gussie was still walking out there, and the sky was so low that it cut off the tips of the mountains. And the sea turned angry. A number of the chalets that peppered the headland were empty. And some had signs sellotaped inside the patio windows – For Rent – with phone numbers.

He wrote each one down on the back of a postcard that had stayed in his coat pocket for weeks. He had bought it in the optimism of the first few days and then couldn't think of anyone to send it to except his mother. He knew there was no going back to school. He knew there was no going back anywhere.

The landlady was only too willing to help him secure a chalet by the beach and he moved in and began living on tins of beans and bags of potatoes. He watched the leaves fall from the trees. He spent the long winter evenings listening to the radio. News shows. Talk shows. Arts shows. Documentaries about wild birds in the sloblands of Wexford. And he rounded off each day with the warm and comforting voice of Daniel O'Donnell singing twenty-three classics from the Jim Reeves songbook on the album *Welcome to My World.*

Daniel O'Donnell was more than a country-and-western singer, with a haircut that said butter wouldn't melt in his mouth. He was an artist. A seducer. He could touch the chord. He could hint at the emotion. He was understated, and he allowed all the emotions to surface in the listener.

Oh Daniel did the job for Gussie! In the privacy of his own little world, Gussie could be anyone he wanted to be, and he played out any fantasy he desired, when Daniel hit the high notes. Yeah. Daniel hit the high notes!

One morning Gussie noticed ice on the roads. The cars were going by with their lights on. What's this? he wondered. And he scrutinized the calendar and realized to his horror that Christmas was just around the corner. It certainly was. And it dawned on Gussie for the first time in his life that Christmas was an obscene and sentimental mess. The log fires and the snow on the television made everyone in the world feel lonely. Including his mother. Though this year he vowed he would not go next or near her. He vowed to avoid that long nightmare of sitting shoulder to shoulder with her in the drawing room, watching Sinatra movies and Bing Crosby movies in stony silence.

Here he was in Connemara at the tail end of November but he didn't quite know what to do instead of going home. The Christmas lights in Cornagore were getting on his nerves. The plastic Santas glowing in the dark. The neurotic version of 'Jingle Bells' in the supermarket. And the voices of little boys in frilly red satin singing 'Ding Dong Merrily on High'.

One afternoon in the grocery shop, he glanced at the rack of tapes and CDs and there in the middle of them all was Daniel O'Donnell sporting a red hat, just like Santa himself. Gussie was shocked. He didn't think Daniel O'Donnell was a man to lower himself to that sort of thing. So after his supper of beans and toast, he took the Daniel O'Donnell tape from the machine and threw it into the rubbish bag, which hung on a knob of the cutlery drawer. He threw Daniel out, and dedicated the night to loud, hot girlie music on the radio.

And he was in luck. He found Sinead O'Connor in concert on Radio One. Two whole hours of Sinead O'Connor. Her anguished voice blasting from the two large speakers, and the ceiling shaking with drumbeats. And he danced in the dark. Christ it felt like dancing with Sinead O'Connor herself. It was that close. I'll give them something to sing about at Christmas, he said to Sinead. But it only felt like dancing with Sinead O'Connor. He wasn't actually dancing with her. It was only a Sinead O'Connor special, recorded the year before in Zurich, the presenter explained in a sweet, cut-glass Dublin accent when the show was over.

He didn't know where Sinead was that night. In a restaurant in Tokyo maybe, with some of her Tokyo pals, drinking sake and having lots of laughs over the raw fish. Or maybe she was at home in her baby-pink pyjamas watching television with a mug of cocoa or giving milk to her baby. Who could tell where Sinead was? One thing for certain: she was not in the wilds of Connemara in a glass wigwam dancing buck naked with Gussie Delaney.

There was a thick pipe travelling horizontally across the ceiling in the bathroom of the chalet, onto which Gussie had attached a secure chain and dog collar. An effective gallows. The chain dangled before his eyes as he sat on the toilet and had a last evacuation. No point in leaving a soiled corpse for the police to be sneering at.

He mounted the rim of the bath and manipulated the chain and collar around his neck. Balancing there naked, and slightly dizzy from the whiskey, he was about to let his weight float into the air, when what does he see but a cat. A dark blur through the fogged glass of the bathroom window. It was Sooty, the neighbours' black cat, with her four white paws, like socks, sitting on the window ledge. He heard her miaow. And then through the open top of the window Sooty stuck in her little head, and stared straight at him.

After that, Christmas was an anticlimax, for both Gussie and Sooty, who took up residence in an orange box beside the fire.

3

ONE OF THE happiest moments that Birdie can recall from Gussie's childhood occurred when the little girl from Italy, on the bus to Galway, opened the cage and released her yellow canary. First it sat on top of the girl's head, and made everyone on the bus fall about with laughter. Then it flew down the bus and landed on Gussie's head. He was nine years old. The canary was pecking his scalp. Such an honour! Being chosen out of all the others. It was like some kind of divine selection. And it was so funny. And whatever salt or oil was in his short hair, Gussie's head was the only skull on the bus that the little yellow bird was bothered with. Birdie and the child walked on air for the rest of the day as they shopped in Galway. Yes. Those were the days alright. A far cry from the seedy bus Gussie ended up on at the age of forty-one.

The seedy Cornagore bus that passed the chalet at two every Thursday heading for Clifden contained a sad army of old men wearing damp coats and hats that resembled tea cozies. Old-age pensioners clutching wicker shopping bags. Gussie travelled on it every week while he remained in Connemara. He'd buy *The Irish Times* in Clifden and read it in the café. Plumes of smoke and steam rising from hot plates of sizzling fish. He'd buy a bottle of whiskey in the off-license and have half a pint of stout in McCabe's bar. All preliminaries of course. All strategies to steady himself before the pilgrimage to the top of the hill.

Some things a mother should never hear. Should never be written. Should never be done. But Gussie did them and by the time the doctors and the social workers, and the psychiatric nurses, were finished with him, Birdie had become privy to her son's most hidden and secret and shameful anxieties. It was like dismembering a butterfly. Except that Gussie didn't seem much like a butterfly. A cockroach perhaps. But not a butterfly. No.

Siobhan Joyce was the butterfly. The girl in the bread shop at the top of the hill. And every week, after his libation in the public house, his tummy fortified with egg and chips, Gussie would make his way to her door with the devotion of a man on the outskirts of Mecca.

Fresh bread was piled like white bricks on the shelves. The floor dusted with flour. Small, white paper bags in neat bundles on the counter. Everything deliciously white. The aroma of cakes baking in the ovens. A door of fogged glass behind the counter, which led to an inner sanctum from which Siobhan came and went. That was another world in there. It was a sanctum beyond his reach. He'd come into the shop with breathless excitement, after ascending the hill. Her shop was at the very top of the street. He'd be puffing. Winded. Unfit. And Siobhan was a glorious brooding presence behind the counter. Seventeen years old. Still uneasy with her great breasts. Long chestnut hair falling over her embarrassed eyes. She dressed in white.

White tee shirt. White trousers. And if she was kneading bread she wore a white apron as well. With pockets where her hands went sometimes for some kind of blue rag she used for dusting her fingers, and wiping droplets of perspiration from her brow.

Gussie was in such a fog of confusion about her that he'd sometimes telephone his mother from the street outside before he went in, and ask her odd questions about his diet as a child.

He could never make up his mind about which bread to buy. And he deliberated too long, so that the young girl became flushed and uneasy. But even that didn't dissuade him. That probably encouraged him. And he'd take all the time he needed to make an impression on her. To demonstrate that he was a man of refined tastes, a man who appreciated her various breads, and her delicate pastries. And thus he stood, gawking, and pointing at things and wondering, while she dusted her little fingers and tried not to breathe. Or maybe she actually knew what he was at. Maybe she realized that the fool fancied he was engaging her with the seductive grace of a civilized gourmet. She was certainly embarrassed. But she may have also felt uneasy. Pinned to the wall while he shifted from foot to foot, prolonging the moment of intimacy with her, and perhaps drooling again as he listened to her breathe.

She found him repulsive. She despised him. Even as he made flirtatious advances. Or what he supposed were advances.

'How's my little Angel Cake today?'

'What have you been cooking for me this week in your little oven?'

Eyeing her with an intense stare that might reveal to her all that craven passion which was building up inside him. Oh, the poor girl.

On the afternoon in question, she could see him coming up the street. She was looking out the window. Later she told it all to the priest. And the sight of him drew from her soul a sigh as mortal as if she was about to throw herself under the lorry passing outside the door. She withdrew to the bakery, behind the door of fogged glass, to recover her composure. Gussie entered. Kicked the slush off his walking shoes at the threshold. Removed his black woolly hat. Opened up with the usual joviality concocted in darkness and solitude. But the shop was empty. There was no one to undress, for the moment.

Then he saw them before his own eyes lying on the counter. A pair of mauve briefs in transparent plastic wrapping. Brand new. Obviously just purchased down the street on her lunch break and idly abandoned for a moment beside a farl of soda bread. His hand hovered. But she sprang suddenly from behind the fogged glass door, snapped up her little item gracelessly, and flung it in the drawer beneath the counter.

'Can I get you anything?' she snapped.

'Bread,' he said, with some disappointment.

That's what she told Father Lee after choir practice the following Saturday evening. She was the last to leave the sanctuary, the guitar still hanging around her neck, and the guitar case still open on the sanctuary floor. She didn't mince her words.

Gussie cooked porridge for himself every morning. It was a discipline that ensured he got out of bed. His daily roughage had become a matter of great importance. He believed that roughage was the answer to the bowel discomforts. But breakfast only brought him to ten o' clock. The rest of the day stretched before him like a terrifying abyss, and he knew that such a gaping emptiness could easily push him back to the excesses of dancing again with Sinead O'Connor. He couldn't always rely on Sooty the cat to save his life, so he invented timetables and strategies to get him through the day.

He divided everything into sections. Times to be out of the house. Times to circulate the juices on a long walk and firm up the rectal muscles that no longer enjoyed the natural firmness of his teenage years. Time for dinner. Time for tea. Time for television. And he saved the pleasure of television for the evenings. It was only a black-and-white set, which he kept hidden in the corner underneath a tartan blanket in case someone might come from the post office looking for a TV licence that he didn't have. So he uncovered it only at night, when the curtains were closed.

This too was risky. Because he fell in love with Sharon on *Home and Away*, a teenage character in an Australian soap opera. He looked forward to it all afternoon, and snivelled into the toilet roll in sympathy with all her little upsets. Sometimes Sharon did bring him to excesses and ledges that equalled his adventures in the toilet with the DIY gallows, but Birdie guessed that the social workers spared her the more disturbing details.

Every Saturday night he cycled to the pub. It was three miles away, down a labyrinth of lanes and past many giant rocks. A tiny pub with a galvanized roof painted green, tucked into the hill at the end of a road that went nowhere else except to the stones of the seashore. There was a concrete floor and a pot-bellied stove. There were old men in damp overcoats and greasy caps. And there was a lady who ran the show and lived in the adjoining house. A lady with a face that suggested frequent bouts of indigestion. She wore a green cardigan too big for her, and she had a chin that would split hailstones. Her son was the image of her. He'd be there sometimes in a navy-blue school blazer and with a Bic biro stuck in his gob as he pulled pints. The scholar. Always on the verge of doing his homework.

The atmosphere varied from one extreme to the other. For weddings and funerals and the infrequent successes of the local drama group in the regional competitions, the little pub became the hub of the world. A junction of nations and emotions. But for the rest of the winter it was empty. Silent. Redolent only with the remorseful sighs of old men clutching the bar and staring bleakly at their pints. Stretching their long necks every time the door opened, as if Grace Kelly might walk in. But their expectation was half-hearted. They had been hardened by lives without surprises.

One night in the cement toilet, an old man was buttoning his urine-soaked coat and staggering from wall to wall. Gussie tried to pass him in the doorway but the old man didn't let him. Instead he hugged him. And Gussie didn't resist. For a second the two men were locked in an embrace.

'Good man yourself,' the old fellow whispered, like a soldier dying. Gussie could feel the piss on his leg. It was seeping from the old man's coat. But yet he hugged him fiercely in desperate solidarity. It wasn't much but it was a moment. That was the first time Father Lee paid Birdie a visit.

'I think he's lonely,' the priest suggested.

Birdie laughed. And then with a smile as inviting as an empty fire grate she said, 'Sure for goodness sake, Father, we're all lonely.'

When the young people came to that pub they came in droves and stuck together. Or they came in flocks and were in and out before anyone could catch them. Or they came when they were least expected, like swallows in a wet April.

And they always arrived like apparitions out of heaven, on the coldest and saddest and most empty night in the year. When the money was spent. When Gussie had polished off his three pints. And he had no more cash in his pocket. And even if he did, he'd have to negotiate with the clock that said midnight, and the long face of the landlady, so terrible that it regularly hunted him out the door.

That's when they came. When the landlady's face was growing longer and longer, as she was clipping up the glasses from empty tables and washing them and drying them and putting them on the shelves with a determination that suggested she might like to close the bar for a thousand years. That's when they came. That's when they arrived. The young people. As if they were from a different planet. Singing laments in Irish about loss and sorrow. Their perfumes driving the old men insane. And of all the flocks and herds and swallows and apparitions, there was nothing quite like the amateur drama group. They'd come at one or two in the morning. With trophies from remote drama festivals in Tubbercurry or Ballyshannon, and they'd stand in a circle and sing songs from American musicals. They'd stand like a flock of geese in the centre of the room, their heads up, their necks stretched. Like geese.

Yes, Father Lee said, they were like geese. But they'd liven up the night. And even long-faced Mrs What-ever-her-name-was couldn't put them out or refuse them drink. Father Lee described it all. He was keeping an eye on Gussie at the time. Father Lee would keep an eye on everyone. He was always there. On the high stool at the far end of the bar.

It was the priest who gave Gussie an old bicycle to get around with. It was he who signed forms so Gussie could collect the dole, when his pay from the school dried up that September. A lean and beautiful priest. Yes. With black hair and thick black brows above his dark Connemara eyes. And didn't Birdie always respect the priests, whether they were beautiful or not?

And he asked no questions. He sang no songs. He stuck to the counter at the far end. His back glued to the wall and his hand rubbing his own knee. An umpire at the match of life, and quietly putting away a long line of little Bacardi and Cokes and watching the world around him, with buckets of tears floating in the air before his face.

One evening in April, just as the light faded from the sky, a blue, watery light, Gussie decided to build a fire in the grate. He was going to fetch more turf from the shed at the back when he was struck by terror. A long lane flanked by giant boulders and heather, and swept by salty gusts from the Atlantic twisted down to the turf shed. Gussie was halfway down when he became aware of a smell. He couldn't place it but it frightened him. It drove him back. It tightened his chest and made his stomach want to heave.

What could he do but retreat to the chalet? It was a cold April evening, and showery. And yet he sat all night at the empty fire grate.

The following morning he realized that the sewage was blocked in the pipes under the chalet and had poured up through a manhole just ten metres from his front door, on the edge of the main road. All that mess, all that pink toilet roll on the roadside, was crying out to heaven. It was Gussie Delaney's waste. His diet. His private stool. Never meant for public inspection. But now it was reeking to high heaven, and the passing cars were splashing through it.

Someone is going to stop and come up to the door of

the chalet, all angry and red in the face and ask him about that! Is this your sewage? Well, it's all over my lovely new Mitsubishi now, and I don't like that. But the one who finally came was Father Lee, with a social worker from Galway. A nice young man with stone-washed blue dungarees, and a rainbow-coloured shirt with no collar. Birdie met him later in the hospital. The two men strolled up the lane and knocked gingerly on the hall door. They had news from the Regional Hospital about his mother.

'It's open,' he called out. 'It's open.'

For Gussie was glad they had come. As they stepped into the hallway, he could see them and they could see him. He was sitting on the toilet with the door ajar, and his trousers around his ankles. He laughed.

'I'll be with yis in a jiffy,' he said.

And he burst out laughing.

'I'm just trying to shit,' he said. And he contorted his face until it swelled and grew red and the jugular sat up on the side of his neck like ivy on a tree.

'Am just trying to shit,' he said. 'Am just trying to shit.'

4

'OH NOW Mrs Delaney, sure you'd be far better off in a nursing home where we could keep an eye on you. Ha ha! Only joking. No but seriously. Think about it. A nursing home near Oranmore, on the Clare road.'

They'd been at it for a year. Gussie was in on it too. Along with the district nurse. And half the fucken staff in the doctor's surgery. And then Birdie got the hip done. That improved things. And Gussie signed himself into a psychiatric ward with bars on the windows. Maybe that too was a sign of improvement. The priest sent word to the chalet in Cornagore, to inform him about the success of the hip, and what does the poor priest find but a man defeated by a sewage pipe.

They replaced the old hip with a new plastic one. And Birdie never felt better. She was scooting around the hospital ward all morning like an ice skater, while out in Connemara Gussie was having a nervous breakdown. One going in and one coming out. That's the way it was that morning. A coincidence weighted with irony. Profound irony. Birdie was well aware what they would say about Gussie's humiliating surrender in his underpants! Lots of juice there for the widows and old ladies who still went to the golf club on Thursday afternoons to sink gin and tonics in the new lounge. Birdie knew from long experience that it's the mother who always gets the blame.

'Oh now, Mrs Delaney, you're not able to be walking around any more with that bad hip.' Then replace it. 'Oh now, Mrs Delaney, would you not lie down and die!' No. 'Well then, what else can we do but find you a nice nursing home, where you'll be safe, and no one will be worrying about you, and we can throw away the key?' Fuck off.

But now it was Gussie who needed to be put away. Ha ha! And to think that he had the neck to be worrying about her. Egging them on! Doing their bidding! It made her blood boil. He even sent her a brochure in the post.

'A tiny room on the second floor of a large complex for elderly tenants, run by the Health Board and private investors.'

The brochure called it exclusive. She would have her

own toilet and shower facility. How lovely. And a television set? You're codding! And a window that looked out on the car park and two lovely birch trees. Shrivelled. The trees were shrivelled. Lovely me arse!

But she humoured Gussie by going to see it. She was breathless in the car. He thought she was going to have a heart attack. He didn't see that it was just the annoyance of being bullied into a prison. Take the shovel and bury yourself. That's what it felt like.

She had to get him to stop the car in Monivea, till she drew her breath in a lay-by beside a scenic wood resplendent with the red and yellow leaves of Canadian maples, but she had recovered enough on entering the glass doors of the reception area to insist on walking upstairs rather than taking the lift. Other residents, with rooms along the same corridor, brought her into their little homes and showed off their fine lace mats, and photographs of their children in Toronto and Seattle, and their silver-framed grandchildren.

Everyone had blue hair. Permed with the fastidiousness of women who spent a lifetime in the golf clubs of Connaught, and couldn't quite understand where the time had gone. The matron was an overweight woman from Longford with military airs. She said she had twins and a husband who farmed near Loughrea. And her bedside manner was straight out of a comedy. She spoke in a loud voice. Did she think that all old people were deaf? She told Birdie there was a red cord hanging from the ceiling in the bedroom. Showed her how to pull it in an emergency. Did she think Birdie didn't know how to pull a string? And there was a common room down the hall where she could play cards and bingo, and listen to local musicians who came in every Tuesday night. Do you dance? she asked Birdie.

Did she think Birdie was a complete fucken idiot? Of course she didn't dance. She was eighty-one years of age.

'Well,' the matron said with a sweet smile, and as if to sum up her wonderful nursing home, 'if there's anything you need, all you have to do is ask.'

Birdie assured her that there was nothing she needed. She never needed anything. She had never put anyone to any trouble ever in her life, and she wouldn't be about to do so now that she already had one foot in the grave. Gussie misread that. He thought she was going to surrender. Thought that his mother was being polite. A sure sign of agreement.

On the way home he talked nonstop about 'your new place' as he called it. He was witless. He had always been witless.

The house Birdie lives in has only one toilet, which is upstairs. And Birdie is fragile on the stairs, especially in the morning when she has dizzy spells. But nobody is going to force her into a nursing home!

Gussie always feared that some day he might find her stuck to the leg of the old sideboard that stood at the bottom of the stairs. If she agreed to go into the nursing home, he contended, she could sit back and watch all her favourite television programmes without worrying about the stairs. And she would have a sit-in shower. A toilet on the same level. No stairs to climb ever again. And a staff of sweetly perfumed nurses to help her wash at any hour of the day or night. According to Gussie, the matron was another Mother Teresa. A vessel of compassion. It's not what Birdie thought. It was a dream come true, Gussie said. Such kindly staff! Such cozy rooms! She would be free, finally, of that big house in the Galway wilderness, with all its moss-infested lawns and dead apple trees, and a forest of nettles in the back garden, and the ancient stables with the broken door, which had to be held in place with two heavy bolts of metal. She'd be free of all that bloody worry, he said.

Well, Gussie is dead now. He's lying in the cold marble sanctuary of the church, waiting for the priest to skite a bit of holy water on him and take him to the cemetery. He's stretched in the oak box that will house him for the next hundred years. Dead as a dead fly.

Little did he know what was up the road. With all his confidence of what the future would be like. All his talk that evening, when they came home to Birdie's house, as he stood in the kitchen, going on and on and on, while the kettle boiled. On and on about how the future was going to be really nice and tidy and Birdie in her snug little nursing home with the fat Mother Teresa administering hourly enemas for the greater comfort of the inmates. He didn't know the future was going to be nice and tidy with him in his little oak box, waiting in the church for the morning gravediggers to plant him six foot under in the hill graveyard.

The day they returned from viewing the nursing home, she just listened and listened, and stared straight ahead as he drove towards Ballinasloe. Until they finally reached her derelict home. The lights of his car lit up the grey stone house and the limbs of the beech trees that surrounded the house. He opened the wrought-iron gate, at the foot of the long avenue, and when he got back into the car he said, 'You'll be glad to leave this place.'

She didn't speak. She opened the front door and went down the hallway, and he followed, and she boiled the kettle in the kitchen, and he was still blathering away, and she made an instant soup in a cup. He refused to have any.

'Oh,' she exclaimed, 'that's going down to me toes.' As

if it wasn't package soup at all. As if the most wonderful thing in the world was being in her own house making her own soup.

'You could make soup there as well,' he said.

She didn't hear him. There was a half-empty porridge package beside the microwave in the kitchen, a walking stick lying on the floor inside the hall door. He went upstairs to the toilet. Through the half-open door of her bedroom he would see the unmade bed, the holy-water bottle, the Virgin Mary on top of the portable television, and the Sunday papers on the floor. It might dawn on him that this was her home.

While he was upstairs in the toilet, she made her decision. The nursing home was a prison. They were all old people in it. What would she be doing with a gang of old people? She was only eighty-one. And the place smelled of lavender. She'd never be able to get rid of that. The perfumes of Arabia couldn't hide what it was: a glorified henhouse for old birds. And what about the grief of walking in and out of each room in her own house for the last time and choosing what to bring with her? She couldn't bear that. They might as well give her the shovel and tell her to dig her own grave. That's what she said. That's what she thought. And Birdie vowed to herself the last big vow of her life. They'll carry me out of here in a box, she whispered at the Sacred Heart of Jesus on the wall.

He was a long time upstairs. When he returned, she said it.

'You were a long time upstairs.'

'I was washing my hands,' he said.

SO WHAT WAS wrong with him, as the neighbours would say? That was the question, wasn't it? She suspected something the year he didn't come home for Christmas. Out in Cornagore swinging from the rafters. And even though Birdie stayed in the house all through January, because of the snow, he never rang. Never rang. Not even a phone call. That's how attached he was to Sooty the cat!

And that winter, Birdie never went out; she was desperately afraid of slipping on the steps of the church, but instead she fell down the stairs one night and sprained her ankle. After that they X-rayed every bone in her body and said that she was a lucky woman. How could it be lucky to fall down the stairs? she wondered.

That was the day the doctor gave her advice on the hip. And she said she'd consider it. So the replacement job was scheduled for the following September. And all through those months, from the sprained ankle in February, right up to the end of August, she never heard from him. How little he thinks of his mother, she thought! He's gone off with a brown cow from Connemara and has no more time for his mammy.

And there was no end to her misery. It never stopped raining. It was windy and cold. She never saw the sun once in July. And for the first time in her life she couldn't even be bothered cooking a little lump of bacon or even a few vegetables for herself. So keen was her sense of foreboding that she agreed to have the last rites before she underwent the hip operation in Galway. But when she woke up and realized that she could walk without a stick or without much pain, her temper improved enormously. She felt young again. And she spoke about her long-dead husband in every second sentence. He'd come into her mind. He'd come like a shadow to the chair beside her hospital bed. He'd come like a ghost into the ward and sit down on the seat across from her. A handsome figure, she told the nurse.

'Hard to make out his features,' she said. 'But it's him.'

The nurses pleaded with her again to consider a nursing home. Especially since her son had been lured into a psychiatric ward. But it was no good. A few days later Birdie headed home to Ballinasloe in the back of a taxi, where she took up residence again on the outskirts of the town, defying old age and infirmity. She paid the driver in coins from her purse. He was a little man from Clare, hardly more than forty, but already grey and puffed in the face, and he whistled all the way as he drove.

'You'll come in and have a cup of tea,' Birdie declared. 'You must be tired from the driving.'

She felt sorry for the pensive way he whistled old waltzes. She herself had a jaunty walk for a woman just over an operation. A black woollen beret cocked to the side of her head. She fumbled for the keys to open the door as they both stood there and the taxi man declared with admiration that she was the picture of health.

'They'll not be burying you for another couple of months,' he chirped.

She didn't think much of that remark but she let him away with it because she had a generally low opinion of taxi drivers and he wasn't the worst. At least he was trying to be cheerful. She sat him in the kitchen like he was a schoolboy, and talked of all the things she was going to get done with the house that she loved. The oil heating wasn't working properly. And she might change the radiators. They were old and bulky and had been there since the time of the Vet. Who was the Vet? the taxi man wondered. My husband, she said coldly, as if he should have known.

The lock on the front door would need replacing. And she was going to get a neighbour who mowed the meadows that surrounded her house to mow her front lawn as well, and put weedkiller on the path, where all the scutch grass and the little wild yellow flowers had been growing all summer. And she had people to tackle. A long list of vendettas that she didn't have the energy for earlier in the year. She had been too worried about Gussie's decline.

'Who is Gussie?' the taxi man inquired. Never mind.

No point in telling the taxi man everything. Gussie was jobless and witless and mired in a confusion of his own making. Wandering around the beaches of Connemara. Locked up in a mental hospital. So who was Gussie? Ha! She didn't know who Gussie was herself any more, though she was hardly going to say that to a stranger. But she said it to the one who understood everything. She whispered it to the Vet. Nobody knows what a mother goes through. Nobody knows the half of it.

'Oh you're right there, Mrs Delaney,' the taxi man agreed, sucking a chocolate biscuit.

Was it Clare he said? Or Longford? It's hard to remember everything. Maybe it was the matron who was the Clare woman. And the taxi man who was from Longford. Or was it the other way about? Was that big fat lump of lard who ran the nursing home from Longford? Anyway, the taxi was halfway down the avenue when the driver, still sucking the remnants of a biscuit, saw her waving. He stopped and reversed until he was beside her. She had forgotten her stick. It was in the back seat. She was laughing like a schoolgirl. He gave it to her and she gripped it in the centre and said, 'Of course I don't need it now, with the new hip!'

You could see he was getting concerned.

'Be careful,' says he, 'and don't be hopping about too much on it. I heard them say at the door of the hospital that you should only walk a little bit every day for the first week or two.'

'And you be careful going back into the city with all that traffic,' she retorted.

'I will, mam,' says he, respectfully, and then, with the car in gear, and his foot on the clutch, he threw her one last glance.

'Jesus, Mrs Delaney,' says he, 'you're a fucken tonic.'

Not much consolation in that was there? To be a tonic for a taxi driver who whistled 'The Tennessee Waltz'? No.

Gussie arrived at her door the following Sunday, with a male nurse who waited in a Nissan Primera outside on the driveway. Gussie walked down the hallway like an old man. He was as stiff as a poker. He stared around the kitchen in gentle bewilderment. Maybe the taxi driver from Clare was bewildered. Maybe most men are bewildered. Maybe it was fortunate that she got the Vet. Maybe she didn't fully appreciate him even now. A man that's not lost in a fog of his own confusion is hard to find and she found the only one who ever walked through Ballinasloe.

So there was no point in Gussie standing in the kitchen looking at her as if he pitied her. He had no fucken right to come into her house and stand there gawking at her like he was trying to figure out who she was. Her grey, wispy hair was standing up in ragged clumps on her head, because she was only out of bed, and her glasses, large headlamps in pink, plastic frames had slipped down her nose. Her eyes had the focused terror of a hunted animal. And around her on the floor were heaps of clothes. Sheets. Blouses. Pyjamas. That was her business. What would he think if she told him about her accident in the bed that morning and having to change everything and wash everything?

By Christ she certainly wasn't going to tell him something like that!

'What's all this?' he asked.

'I'm spring-cleaning.'

He sneered.

'It's October.'

She stared at him and he looked away. But it was him who was almost on the verge of tears.

'What's the matter with you?'

'It's intolerable,' he blurted out.

'What?'

'Intolerable that you're here on your own, with no one to look after you. People are worried.'

She could have told him there and then that she had plenty to look after her. She could have stuck her wedding finger under his nose and told him that the day she undertook to wear that band of gold, she got someone to look after her who had never let her down and was still minding her. And then he'd think she was daft. Yes. Isn't that funny? Him worried about her being daft. The pot calling the kettle black.

'Where's your car?' she demanded.

'What?'

'I said where is your car?'

He said he didn't have one any more. No. He didn't. And why not? Why did he not have a car any more? She was getting into her courtroom rhetoric, the voice gradually rising, the rage coming to full throttle. Why?

'I sold it,' says he.

Yeah. He had sold it. Ladies and gentlemen of the jury, he sold his car. And why does a man sell his car?

'Because I have no job at the minute. You know that.'

Exactly! 'Because he has no job at the minute.' And now let us proceed. Who is the geezer at the front door? Who is that boy outside my front door, dozing in his fancy big car?'

'You know who it is. I've explained about the hospital.'

'Yes,' she said. 'You have already explained.' She left a pause. A long pause. A delph-rattling, earth-shattering pause. And then, a thousand years later, she added a whisper, 'It's yourself, Gussie, you should be worried about now. Not me.'

6

HE HAD BEEN there before. In Connemara. Years ago. When he was a child. He went to the Irish summer college, to learn the language by mixing with the native speakers. Birdie has found the photographs. She can pick them from behind the cellophane of a leather photo album and hold them at a distance to make out the faded details. Where are they? Here they are! All the Polaroids he had taken home with him.

But what is that noise? And where is she? It takes a second but yes, Birdie is in the bed. It's the middle of the night.

So naturally she wonders about a strange noise. She listens again. It's coming through the wall. It's the sound of someone in the next room. Someone waking before their alarm perhaps? Someone going to the toilet maybe? No. It's nothing like that. It's probably the Vet walking about in the other world. That's what it is. Yes. The Vet.

It's that kind of night. Silent and windless. And it's nowhere near dawn and her feet are cold.

She raises herself out of the bed. Stands erect. Wobbles. Leaves the room. Negotiates the stairs, one at a time and goes down to the front room that looks out on the lawns and the avenue. Stooping carefully, she plugs in the two-bar heater and sits on the sofa.

But she has forgotten the leather photo album. So she must go back up the stairs. A long slow ascent until she is back once more in the bedroom. And there it is lying on the duvet. OK. Now back down the stairs. Gingerly. Gingerly. Down one at a time. Bit of a wobble. Stop. Sit. First move the feet. Now move the bum. And again move the feet. And again move the bum. Until finally, exhausted, she lands down on the bottom step, clutching her leather album. And she walks back into the drawing room where the two-bar heater has warmed up the room and she can put her feet up close to toast her toes. But they're not cold now. They have already warmed up from all the travelling up and down. Up and down like a fucken yo-yo.

She sits on the sofa and stares at her pictures. Cornagore 1966. The beach. Four little boys staring at the camera lens. Gussie at the edge, all lanky and frowning. That's where it all started. And perhaps that is why he went back? Perhaps that is why he spent half the year pacing the beach like someone lost from a wrecked ship.

Gussie was a shy child who could not tie his shoelaces or make a knot in his tie. He was a dribbler and a gazer. His shirts and jumpers were layered with days of dried egg, tomato ketchup, tea and milk, and green snot from his nose, which he cleaned by wiping on the sleeve of his jumper.

It was two o'clock in the afternoon. A warm August afternoon. Gussie was in a house in Cornagore with a few other boys. All students at the summer school. And the woman of the house announced to the five little scholars that she was going to the village for sausages and would return at five o'clock to make their tea. She quizzed them through the door of the bedroom. She was meticulous at not intruding on their privacy, but she persisted at the door for a long while. Surely they had language classes in the afternoon? No. Or maybe dancing classes or singing classes? No. But the summer school could hardly be closed down for the day, she persisted. The landlady knew that. There must be something on for the students in the afternoon.

Long pause.

Imagine the landlady standing outside the little bedroom where the five boys were stretched on their bunk beds, and maybe she's thinking to herself that this is a little fishy. Very well then, she suggested, they might like to walk with her into the village. If they met one of the teachers, they could check. That didn't go down too well. Not an option at all, they said. In fact they couldn't. Because they all had sick tummies. Everybody? Yes. From what? Who knows? Ice pops! And some had headaches. From walking in the wind, because it's windier in Connemara beside the ocean than anywhere else in Ireland. And now they declared that they all had permission from the teachers to take the afternoon off as long as they stayed in bed. The landlady gave up. It was almost half-two by now and she had a long walk for her sausages.

And as regards the little boys in their bedroom, the rest is a tale of innocence unveiled. But for Gussie, it was the terrible shock of a first kiss. And the landlady was no eejit. She reported everything to the teachers and the teachers reported it back to the parents. Which is how Birdie found out. And how it had lodged like a stone in her chest for years, when she'd look at him growing up. Imagine Gussie brushing his lips against the other boys' lips. Doing things that probably returned to haunt him for years.

You see he wasn't a girl, was he? If he was a girl, he might have remained calm and silent in the afterglow of that first kiss. Or brushed his lips on the back of his new master's neck. The aftertaste of first love still on the tongue. But he wasn't a girl. Was he? No. Of course not. Birdie was a girl. Is. Yes. Is a girl. She would have known what to do. But boys! You can't be up to them. And you can't rely on them. And when there's music in the air, they walk on your toes.

Gussie didn't do any of the things he ought to have done if he was a girl, or if Birdie was him, or if everybody was somebody else. He didn't do all the things he saw later in films on solitary visits to London. He didn't even lie still. No. Couldn't even do that. Had to be the circus clown. Had to make a show of himself. Had to be the gobdaw.

A convent girl might have stayed still, and learned a thing or two and if she didn't like it she might just have spilled the beans on the bastards later. Then of course a convent girl wouldn't be in a room with four boys. So there's no point in thinking that.

Who knows? It's late in the night. Gussie is dead. He has no more chances. And all Birdie knows is that, far from being the victim, because he was the youngest, the one they took advantage of, Gussie managed to turn himself into the ringleader.

By the end of the day it certainly looked like that. He

45

danced and pranced around the room. He jumped up and down on the floor. He made a mighty entertainment for the other kids as they lay on their wet, steamy bellies reeking of childish sweat and sex. Gussie was the star. The eejit. The gobdaw. And they applauded him with the enthusiasm of an audience in the town hall watching the village beauty dancing the can-can in the opening chorus of a Christmas pantomime. But the ructions drew the attention of the landlady's daughter, who drank her fill through the keyhole and blew the whistle that evening at teatime with unrestrained glee.

Gussie was sent home. He was the one who had started the whole thing, the teachers said. And the landlady said. And the other boys said. Excuse me, said Birdie, but what age is my son? And what age are all the other bastards? So on and so forth. But it was useless.

It was an incident never repeated but often recalled. Connemara was a word that exploded in the air whenever it was uttered. If she didn't like where he was going or what he was doing, she'd say I hope it's not going to turn out like Connemara. When her heart was utterly black and she wanted to flail him to pieces, she simply said, I hope this is not going to be another Cornagore.

And then that summer came along. The time after the incident with the schoolgirl in the chipper and he announced that he was going on his holidays and she thought fine, let him go, he might enjoy a bit of fun in some nice sunny climate with a few of his teacher friends. But then he said the word. Cornagore. Sacred Heart of Jesus, what did he say? Yes. Cornagore. He was off to Cornagore. For what? For a holiday.

A lot of blather then about getting some personal space for himself and relaxing and finding himself. And he was only staying the night with Birdie. And he was off to Cornagore in the morning. She didn't take her eye off the television for an hour. She glued herself to rubbish. Stupid comedy programmes just to avoid what she might say to him if she looked at him.

At ten o'clock he said he'd go into town for a pint.

'Don't take the car,' she said. 'You never know when the guards are on the road with that breathalyzer thing. And the walk might do you good.'

Yeah. Well it didn't. He had four solitary pints in the hotel. He was slouched against the edge of the bar as the young nurses and teachers assembled at the beginning of their Friday night out. And with each pint he grew more agitated. More conscious of his solitude haunting their happy company. Eventually he walked back to his mother's house in a state of despair and gave her an account of his evening out. She was still watching the end of *The Late Late Show*.

He slept over and in the middle of the night he heard the lowing of cattle, so close that he thought they were downstairs. In fact they were out in the garden, and his mother was on the landing, the track of a hairnet as deep as a tyre-burn across her forehead, and wearing a pink dressing gown all the way down to her white ankles.

'The rose bushes, the rose bushes, your father's good rose bushes.'

'Jesus Christ, Mother, they're only fucken rose bushes,' he screamed, 'but whenever anything comes under attack from cattle breaking into the garden, you invoke Daddy's name in a trance like a saint invoking the name of the fucken unknowable God.'

That was a quare speech. He was raging and he was in his pyjamas. No. In his pyjama tops, and Birdie, having no time to discuss other options, was exposed to the sight of his white rump flying across the landing and down the stairs, reducing her to a rare state of silence.

He ran around the rose beds with his pyjama top flying, in a desperate effort to get the cattle out the gate. But that so frightened one particular cow, who became as nimble on her pins as a ballerina, that she pranced and leaped everywhere to get away from him, including onto the bonnet of his new Ford Escort. And Gussie in a blistering rage, and without his trousers, was vulnerable in the brutal world. The outcome was that he came through an unseen bramble of rose bush in the dark and almost destroyed himself. Birdie waited until he was halfway up the stairs before addressing him.

'I only hope nobody saw you,' she said. And she withdrew like a queen from the scene of a slaughter, and closed her door with a gentleness that wouldn't disturb a mouse. Gussie bathed his cuts and then went to his bedroom to lie on his bed in agony and shame. She was trying not to think of his white rump on the landing. Trying not to think of Cornagore. That terrible kiss, still as fresh as recently baked bread. And she knew Gussie still sustained himself on that. Always digesting it with a garnish of savage nostalgia. Someone might as well have locked his penis in a box and hung it on a tree, where he could never get at it again.

Birdie too lay awake in her room, listening to the BBC World Service at maximum volume. With maternal clarity she could hear him breathe and she supposed that she could hear him think. But what she couldn't do was go into his room and put her arms around him ever again. And she certainly can't do it now. Because he's dead.

THE VET

I

BERNADETTE. That was Birdie's name. And her daddy brought her to Dublin on the steam train. And from that day, and ever since, she loved the flutter of a bird's wing. And that first magical encounter with birds, on a street outside the railway station, orchestrated by a beggar woman, became a bond between herself and Daddy. It was a sign of his ultimate fidelity. It excused everything. Because he was doing his best for her, in those years after her mother died. And every winter she fed the same little robin with crumbs and lard from the kitchen table.

What a day! Standing there at eleven years of age, with ten or twenty white pigeons flitting about her head. And afterwards on the train home Daddy whispered in her ear. 'They were like angels from heaven,' he said.

She could see he was enchanted. She could see that he too was thinking about Birdie's mammy. Birdie can remember how he held her up on the platform. The great iron skirts of the engine dripping wet and the clouds of steam enveloping everyone on the platform in Ballinasloe.

Daddy always lifted her up like that. He was a big man.

And he moved slowly, like a lion in the forest. He played poker and had carrot-coloured whiskers and drank only on rare occasions, but when he did he could put the house upside down. He never smiled after his wife died.

It was Daddy who first called her Birdie. She'd be sitting up in bed. Nervous of the dark. Her fragile body as straight as an ash sapling. Her limbs as taut as the strings of a fiddle. Her head cocked. Her eyes searching the edge of the room for anything that might be moving in the shadows.

'My little Birdie,' he'd whisper.

And since she had no brothers or sisters, she was eventually left minding this big whale of a man with a bad chest who could hardly breathe for the last four years of his life as he went blue in the face and wheezed in the kitchen of the little cottage on St Martin's Terrace.

By the time she was thirty the people of St Martin's Terrace had crowned her Queen of all Spinsters. Boiling pots of lard and suet to feed the birds and reeking of carbolic soap after the hours she spent soaking her daddy's blisters were all signs of self-neglect, they said. If it wasn't for the birds, the house would be full of cats. Cobwebbed knickers. Mothballed petticoats. No two ways about it. She was already a spinster.

There were others said that she set her sights too high in the early years. They said her father was only a cattle drover. He had no land. No shop. And there were plenty of boys in the terraces and the cottages on the outskirts of the town who might have made her a good husband. But she turned her nose up at them, didn't she? All of them. As if a coalman or a lorry man or a man who made a living from manicuring the gardens of the professional classes was somehow not good enough for Bernadette Waters.

And then Birdie proved them all wrong. She caught

the biggest fish in town. In the autumn of 1953 Bernadette Waters appeared in the *Connaught Tribune*, grinning from ear to ear with a bouquet of flowers in one hand and Alex Delaney, bachelor of Cork city, veterinary surgeon, and former captain of Kilmallock Golf Club, in the other. 'Hand in hand' the caption said above the photograph. There's swank for you now! The life of the golf club beckoned for Bernadette Waters.

The newly married couple moved into a lovely big house on the outskirts of the town, and off the main road, in the quiet rolling fields of east Galway where the ditches were clean jumps for horses and the mature beech trees made copses on every hillside.

The house was an elegant monument to the aspirations of Galway gentry in the nineteenth century. A detached dwelling, in grey stone, it went for a song to Mr Delaney from Cork, who had it re-roofed, pebble-dashed and painted blue, so that it became a posh love nest for Birdie and the Vet. The meadow between the house and the road was dug up, re-soiled and re-seeded to become a green lawn, where children might play croquet at a safe distance from rough neighbours, or the brats who cursed up and down the terraces of the town all summer long. Birdie and the Vet were away from the road. All alone on the verdant lawn.

The transformation was sudden. The lawn was so green and the pebble-dash so blue that the townsfolk would stroll out the road on a Sunday afternoon just to admire it from a distance. A posh paradise for Birdie Waters from the terraces whose marriage was an event that caused more astonishment locally than the Shah of Iran's recovery of Persia.

Birdie's wedding album has cream covers as soft as sponge, and it's still wrapped in the original cellophane.

She has a special place for it at the back of the wardrobe in a box and she is thinking about it as she plugs out the heater, and closes the drawing-room door and climbs the stairs once again. The night is endless.

She intends to take out the wedding album and lay it on the bed and open it. Perhaps that will help her sleep. But halfway up the stairs she remembers that she has left the black leather album in the drawing room. Isn't that what she was doing? She was looking at photographs. So she turns on the stairs and begins the descent again.

But not more than a step or two before she halts. She's trying to remember something. What?

Oh yes. She remembers. It's the other one, isn't it? It's the other album.

The one downstairs is the leather one; not the white photo album. It's not the wedding one. No. The wedding one is still in the bedroom. At the back of the wardrobe. So she wheels around again. Faces up. Ascends. Christ it's not easy when you're old. Bad enough going up or down once. But now she is up and down like a yo-yo, because she forgets things. That is not good. Not good at all.

Anyway, here she is now in the bedroom. Yes. But did she plug out the heater? That's another question. Maybe she did. At least she pretends she did.

And here, in the bedroom, in the wardrobe, it finally comes out.

Now look at that! Such a treasure! Folded in soft tissue paper and sitting at the bottom of a cardboard box that contained the fairy lights the Vet bought for their first Christmas, half a century ago. Yes. Here is the best album, full of all her most important memories, waiting for her arthritic fingers to touch.

Gussie had a frightened look as a child. His tie hanging loose. The sides of his shirt sticking out. An uncertainty in the expression. As if the camera was penetrating him.

As a boy he dreaded walking down the street of his hometown where he would be interrogated by pensioners who would pull his ears for no reason at all. There was a madman on a walking stick who travelled the town by feeling the walls. And a blind man behind sunglasses at the door of the public house. There was a fat man who sat on a kitchen chair on the pavement outside the door, a blanket over his knees, his pipe and glasses resting on the local newspaper at his feet, as he closed his eyes and stretched his face to the fitful bursts of the sun on a cloudy day in June. Always pretending he was asleep.

'And who are you?'

'Gussie.'

'Ah! You're a child of Birdie Waters.'

'That's right.'

The old man rubbed his callused hand across the child's hair, as if he was combing it. As if he was searching the soft flesh of a lamb before plunging in the knife. But let's not dwell on that. No. Not now.

For now she turns the page and opens the book of her wedding day.

And she can see him. Alex. The very first photo. With the cigarette in the side of his mouth and that smirk on his face. That Fred Astaire pose against the side of the car. Oh Christ, he could be handsome when he wanted to.

Alex Delaney was the Vet who came from Cork and lodged in a red-bricked boarding house with Arthur Murphy, a man who worked in the bank and had bad breath and later went on to be a government minister. There was another boarder as well but he had no significance for the young ladies. An older man who was bald and managed the local cinema and played the organ in the church. He had been in the boarding house so long nobody knew where he had come from. Or if he had come from anywhere. Perhaps he was from the town and owned the boarding house. Birdie can't be expected to remember everything about everyone. She remembers the Vet. That's enough.

He was a tall man. Slim and obscure. He had a light heart and a light foot, and when he first arrived in Ballinasloe the townspeople were of the impression that he was a flirt whom nobody would ever tie down. He was in his late forties, and wore grey linen suits and soft felt hats, and when he smoked his cigarettes the girls said he looked like an American in a film. His arrival in town was an enormous event in the social calendar. Vets were the men of the future, people said. Farming was going to be called agriculture. Bulls were going to be abolished. It would all be coming out of a test tube in a laboratory. Everything would become scientific. And the vets were the boys who had the road maps.

He arrived. Oh he did surely. In a big Austin Morris station wagon. Or was it a Ford? Anyway. He sang the 'Banks of My Own Lovely Lee' in the discreet snug of Mannion's Bar where the professional men went drinking on Friday nights. He wasn't afraid to let go. But as people said, that kind of thing is alright in Mannion's if you have the money behind you. And though everybody guessed that Alex Delaney didn't have much then, they knew that in time he would. He was a man who knew the future, they said. He saw what was coming. He was like a man waiting for apples to fall off the tree, they said.

Dumbstruck. That's the only word could describe the reaction of all the virgins of Ballinasloe, the daughters of the shopkeepers, and the teachers and traders, with their piano lessons and their convent educations. Dumbstruck. That's the truth. When he married Birdie Waters. And it wasn't just her address in the terraces. It was the lines on her face. The mileage on the clock, as they said. Birdie was no chicken.

But they were married anyway, and not in the big church in the town, with pomp and fanfare, but in a small country chapel on the edge of the parish; on a hill a few miles from the town and Birdie didn't even wear a wedding dress. She wore a pleated suit in pale blue, with a matching hat like a small fez. It was modern and caused people to say with envy that she looked like an air hostess.

Then they had breakfast in Hayden's Hotel, with all the family. And that's when Hughie Donoghue turned up. Hughie was the Vet's first friend in town. A chain smoker with the soft Mayo accent and hair like Elvis Presley, a long, angular face, with enormous hands and long ivory fingers. That was the important thing. The fingers. He used to joke that he had them insured, on account of the flute.

He was a flute player at a time when musicians were barely tolerated, rarely allowed to play, and considered as hardly more than a step above tinkers, criminals and imbeciles. So that was Hughie. And that was the picture of Hughie that Gussie saw when it fell out on the floor. Hughie Donoghue. Dattledo Donoghue.

It was the day on which Gussie first suggested to his mother that she should be thrown into a nursing home. A dustbin. She glared at him and then just walked out of the kitchen and went upstairs without uttering a word.

He heard her crying. She was whimpering. Softly. Like a child. So he went upstairs after her, and she was on the landing, holding the door handle of her room, as if she feared someone might be about to drag her physically away forever. When she calmed down, she went into the bedroom and rummaged in the wardrobe until she found the wedding album. She sat on the bed leafing through it for consolation, tears streaming down the white blotting-paper skin of her cheeks. Gussie tried to reason with her but she told him to go away. And then a photo of the flute player fell out of the album and Gussie picked it up.

'Who's this?'

Well he knew bloody well who it was. He knew Hughie Donoghue. Everyone in Galway knew Hughie. Hughie was one of those public characters, like a landmark or a bend on the road that everyone connects with eventually. Everyone had their own Hughie Donoghue story.

Birdie just said Hughie was his father's friend. And she snapped the picture from him, and returned it carefully to its place behind the cellophane. Then she leafed over another few pages until she found pictures of Gussie when he was a baby in huge woollen cardigans and woollen hats, as if they all lived in Iceland.

That got rid of him. One glance at those and he was gone from the bedroom, and down the stairs. Couldn't bear those images of himself as a baby.

Who is he? says Gussie. For Jesus' sake! Did he think Birdie was a half-wit or what? Or maybe he thought Birdie was losing her mind at the time. Yes. That's it. He thought Birdie was going gaga, and gawking at photos of her marriage without remembering what her own name was. And then he'd have her all wrapped up for the dustbin in a jiffy.

Boys oh boys, but he was barking up the wrong windmill that day, if that's what he thought.

Birdie could quote chapter and verse about Hughie Donoghue. Then or now. He was a flute player who lived halfway up a mountain, outside the village of Crosshill, which itself was ten miles beyond Ballinasloe. He used to hitch lifts and he'd go wheresoever the lift was going. He'd stand on the roadside maybe hitching southwards, until he heard a car coming. Sometimes the car might be going northwards. So he'd cross the road and hitch northwards. He never actually cared where he was or where he was going, so long as he was always going somewhere. And once he got the drivers' attention, he could stick to them like glue for the entire day and night. People said there was a trace of a tinker in him, and he never disagreed. And his nickname was Dattledo Donoghue.

'Where are you going?' he'd inquire. But no matter what the driver replied, Hughie would sing his tune – 'That'll do.'

'Where are you going?'

'Clifden.'

'That'll do.'

It didn't matter what the driver said.

'Where are you off to?'

'Castlebar.'

'That'll do.'

Flexible Donoghue.

'Where are you for, sir?'

'Timbuktu.'

'That'll do.'

If his dog was sick, he'd get the neighbour to drive him to town, to see the Vet. Or sometimes, in more recent years, when his bones were stiff and the cod liver oil wasn't working, he'd oblige a neighbour to make the trip to north Mayo or south Roscommon, so he could visit some quack or faith healer, or Dutch hippie practising reiki, or maybe a German woman in Sligo who massaged arthritic farmers with a concoction of beeswax and wild nettles.

Those trips took forever. They were adventures. Especially when he was in favour of approaching the German woman with the nettles. They'd stop at every pub on the way to and from Sligo. Always on the pretext of getting directions.

And they'd have a pint in each pub they passed until eventually they hit on a musical house. Then Hughie would be drawn into the session. The driver got techy. The dog slept in the back of the car.

The driver would recount such stories to Alex Delaney over some calving cow a week later and Birdie would hear it on the pillow from the inebriated Vet.

And always the same groceries. Rashers and sausages and a sliced pan. Hughie never went home without the essentials. And in the laneway to his house he'd cajole the driver to come in for a feed. And the food would be served with lashings of Powers Gold Label whiskey. A stock of bottles Hughie kept out in the shed. It was ancient whiskey, bonded by a local pub fifty years earlier. Incomparable to any other whiskey in the world. And when the driver finally let his ears back to the feast of bacon and fried bread, Hughie would settle himself by the range and render hornpipes and polkas on the flute. Tunes tunes tunes, until the cows came home. Tunes as clear and sweet as brown trout in a stony river. As Hughie used to say, sure there's no tomorrow. There's only today.

Many's the driver agreed, repeating the mantra – there's

no tomorrow – as they turned off the engine and went inside for that feed. The small cottage with its green, galvanized roof humming all night until the clear light of dawn. Though in latter years the supply of special whiskey ran out and the music suffered from a lifetime of smoking Sweet Afton.

There were snooty bitches who raised their eyebrows at a man like the Vet mixing with the likes of Dattledo Donoghue, but for goodness sake it was the most natural thing in the world. The Vet from Cork needed to get around the countryside in a hurry. The job took Alex up highways and down laneways. It was always an emergency. There were no maps of the by roads in those days, and the back end of east Galway was a maze of untarred lanes, crossroads without signposts, and T-junctions in the middle of nowhere. He needed to find bulls and calving cows, and horses with chest infections. And nothing suited Hughie more than a long summer's day in the Vet's old station wagon, his dog looking out the rear window, and the Vet singing ballads from Cork, as they whizzed along between the bramble ditches, turning this way and that way in accordance with Hughie's masterful directions.

While Alex was poking in some cow's rear end, Hughie was in the kitchen talking to the wife, or searching for some fiddle player who lived a few fields farther on.

In the time before tape recordings, the musicians always greeted each other with special joy, like long-lost comrades, and Hughie was able to pick up new tunes wherever he went. In fact, he was as welcome as the Vet ever was on their travels, because he had all the tunes. No one at the time was travelling more of the west than Hughie. So no one had more tunes. And the more tunes he had, the more he got.

Have a cow – get a cow. Have a tune – get a tune. Same story. People said he had over five hundred polkas alone in his head and fingers.

So he was invited to the wedding. It wouldn't have been thinkable to keep him away. Even if Birdie's daddy did have a problem with him.

Dattledo and Daddy had a history. Oh yes. Daddy treated musicians with the same caution as people treat journalists nowadays. At least the tabloid journalists. And for much the same reason. Musicians were notorious for recording the sordid details of all weddings or funerals. If there was dirt, then the balladeers could rake it up.

Years earlier when Daddy was burying his wife in Mayo someone in the pew behind him remarked that if the lady hadn't met Waters, she might be still alive. Nobody required the newspaper to tell them whom Daddy had hit in that blind fit of rage. Or how he had taken a candlestick off the altar and clapped it into the full face of his wife's brother, drawing blood in squirts from the victim's nose, which sprinkled the congregation like holy water, and fell like flecks of pepper on the cream habit of the deceased woman, as she lay stretched in an open coffin. Nobody required photographs of the priest in his black and white vestments flapping about like a deranged penguin trying to calm the fracas. Nobody required a newspaper report of the proceedings, because within a week the entire funeral was sung, verse-by-verse and blow-by-blow in every pub from Belmullet to Castlebar. Daddy couldn't stand musicians after that. It made no odds that Donoghue didn't know the song. As far as Daddy was concerned, all musicians were guilty.

The last verse in particular cut Daddy to the bone, highlighting the fact that his wife's final written request was that she be taken back to Mayo and buried with her own people. She was leaving her husband alone to gasp his way to the single grave that awaited him in the cemetery near Ballinasloe. A sort of bleak divorce that Birdie often wondered about.

And look. There's the picture of Daddy at the church gate. Mr Waters, manoeuvering his enormous body out of the black taxi. And in the photographs she can see the side of Dattledo's face. He was smoking a Sweet Afton and leaning against the railings, hoping for a signal to join the party. But there was a big scowl on Daddy's face that wasn't difficult to interpret. Stay the fuck away from my daughter's wedding. That was the message.

Hughie had no intention of doing anything of the kind, for he was acting on alternative instructions. He remained on the doorstep of the church for the entire ceremony and he haunted the bar of Hayden's Hotel later on, while the relations were upstairs enjoying a breakfast of duck eggs and ham at the expense of the old cattle drover.

When the cake was cut, Daddy rose like lord of all he surveyed and smiled a blessing on everyone present. He said his piece and then handed his daughter over to 'the man from God knows where' as he called Alex Delaney. And he declared how much he loved his only child. And how happy he was that this day had dawned, and that she had found her heart's desire.

She was always a stubborn girl he said. But on this occasion he approved of her choice. She had waited. Stubbornly waited, and she had been wise to wait. For she was not prepared, says he, to take any old teddy boy from Ballinasloe. No. The Waters were no ordinary drovers, says he. They were dealers. Great dealers. They knew their meat. Murmurs of moral approval rose from the long table of relations who supposed themselves to be a step above buttermilk, now that one of their own had captured the Vet from Cork.

Then Mr Waters excused himself, saying that owing to his unfortunate chest, which felt like it was lying under an anvil, he must urgently retire from the festivities for a while. It was only when he had left the building and walked down the street with Birdie on his arm that Dattledo got out the flute and started things going with a pair of gentle little hornpipes he had heard in Banagher.

The fact is that the virgins of Ballinasloe didn't think she'd catch anything. Couldn't catch a fucken cold, she couldn't! At her age! Not a trout in the river for her, they hoped. Certainly no one expected her to catch Fred Astaire, as they called the Vet. And them still whispering his name to their pillows long after his wedding. The virgins with their piano lessons and the shopkeepers' daughters with their repressed desires. Oh Birdie knew what they were saying about her. Even on her own street, she knew what was said by those who called themselves friends. And it was on account of what she knew that she escorted her daddy to the door of his little terraced cottage, and then walked back up past Fahey's sweet shop on the corner and marched in triumphantly, and displayed her prize to Colette Fahey. The big stone and the gold band around her wedding finger. She shoved it all the way up under Colette's nose and said, 'Now, Colette. Take a good look at that. Isn't it only gorgeous?'

And Colette declared that, as God was her judge, she had never seen such an enormous ring. And she wished Birdie luck. And happiness. Wasn't it a charity, and a sweet reckoning to make Colette spit all that out. Not that there could be the slightest bitterness on a day like that. She even said to Colette to come up later to the party. And Colette said she might put her head in the door for a minute, when she was finished in the shop. It was going to be the mother and father of a party, Birdie promised. And she wasn't lying.

The music did indeed put a jaunt in the day. Like beetles, one musician attracted another. And it was hardly past noon when the sound of hornpipes and reels in the bar of Hayden's Hotel attracted Tommy Curtin, the box player from Menagh, and John Joe Curley, the fiddle player from Garvay, who were in on their bikes for the messages, and were sitting not two doors away, in Henderson's, a little newspaper shop where all the countrymen used to congregate in the old days, sitting on upturned biscuit tins and orange boxes, and smoking their Woodbines, and talking to old stiff Henderson, when they couldn't afford to go into the pubs.

By five o'clock that evening the session had filled out with musicians from everywhere. Christ, it was turning into a national cultural event, Birdie thought. Musicians from the four provinces, all dropping in one at a time, as if it was all by accident, and not a subtle choreography resulting from the Vet's connivance with Hughie, and Hughie's diligent efforts over six months up and down the shores of the Shannon, advising musicians of the spree there would be on the day of Birdie's wedding in the hotel in Ballinasloe.

By eight o'clock they were all moved into a large function room. A special bar was opened. The musicians struck up a waltz. It filled the smoky room under the low rafters, and the dancing was begun without the slightest deference to the bride, who by tradition ought to have been the first on the floor. But she didn't seem to mind, for at one stage, when the musicians were having a break, she was seen in earnest conversation with Hughie Donoghue as his flute rested on the table beside his pint and he leaned his head forward, so that she could whisper in his ear.

By midnight hardly anyone present, dancing or drinking or playing music, could quite remember what occasion had triggered such a fantastic session, and Alex Delaney and Birdie Waters were upstairs in the Number One bedroom, sitting on either side of that enormous creaking mattress, declaring their hearts to each other, telling each other the secrets of a lifetime, and promising the rest.

Alex had a lot to tell. And Birdie never repeated what he told her to another living soul. But then Birdie had her own little secrets too. Hadn't she? And the pale light of dawn was not far away when they both finally collapsed into each other's arms, and discovered their own unique moment of bliss on the springs of a big fancy bed.

2

ALTHOUGH IT WAS September, the morning sunshine was intense. And it spilled in through the window, on to the linen tablecloth and the cream porcelain china of the breakfast table in Hayden's Hotel. It was a huge dining room sinking into a soft paisley-patterned wool carpet.

The whole thing was hushed and splendid. Like a spring morning. And the sunshine warmed Birdie's shoulder blades, for which she was thankful to the most merciful Christ, since she had decided on a light-blue cotton dress that morning, in the excitement of waking up beside the Vet on the first day of the rest of their lives. In the yard outside, Alex showed her the new car. It was the Ford. Or maybe not. Maybe it was the white Austin station wagon.

That was it. He came in a Ford. Then he got rid of it before the wedding. Yes. Birdie cannot be sure about things like that.

But she remembers him opening the door. He had hidden the car at the rear of the hotel as a surprise for her. He was fussing like a magician all morning. Until the big event. The big trick in the car park.

'You could go to Dublin and back in that,' he asserted, 'and you'd not have to worry about breaking down.'

Maybe it was the Ford? No. It was the white station wagon. That was the big rabbit in the hat, so to speak. And certainly it was a huge surprise for Birdie.

But not for Hughie Donoghue. He had slept in it for the few short hours that remained of the night after the night porter had locked the drinks cupboard and began mopping up the sawdust floor of the bar with a bucket of foul-smelling disinfectant.

It must have been the station wagon because Dattledo Donoghue was lying in the back of it. Stretched. Like a corpse in a white hearse. Birdie was standing back to admire the car and she held her hands to her cheeks, as she saw the girls do in films when the hero presents them with something wonderful. But then she let out a shriek of horror when she saw the corpse. Or rather the long, bony face of Hughie Donoghue staring out at her through the back window where he had been stretched all night underneath his black coat. He smiled at her a wounded little smile on the bottom half of his long face. And he said hello.

There was a pear tree growing up a stone wall on one side of the yard. Birdie never forgot that pear tree. It was flush with ripe little pears as small as plums and it gave Birdie something to do as Alex removed Hughie from the car and got him on his way. Or so she hoped. But she hoped in vain.

When the negotiations were over, Hughie had convinced Alex that Kerry was such an astonishing land of music that it would be a crime against art to leave him behind.

'If you only get me as far as Tralee,' says he, 'I'll make me own way home.'

And she didn't argue. It didn't really matter who came with them on their honeymoon, so long as Alex was driving and the sun was shining. That's all she needed, because the world was different that morning. She had entered the infinite security of knowing that there was someone to make all the decisions in her life from now on. She firmly believed that Alex, being a vet, and being from Cork, and being an exquisite dancer who could probably drive all the way to Kerry and back without once looking at a map, was entirely correct in choosing to bring a flute player.

As it turned out, he wasn't far wrong. Everybody got on famously well. The third party in the group prevented either Alex or Birdie from being overwhelmed by four long days of isolated intimacy.

So off they go. The two of them in the front of the white hearse, and the dead flute player stretched in the back. It's a huge hearse now, and the flute player is getting longer and longer, so that his feet stick out the rear window, and she's saying to Alex, is this the Ford or is it the white station wagon?

At last he answers her. His head floats through the wall from the other world, and he calls her. Birdie. Birdie. You're dreaming!

Birdie wakes up with a fright. Yes. She was dreaming. There she is in the bed. And the light is off. It's dark. And she fumbles around under the pillow for her flashlight. It's working. So she points it at the bed. Moves the beam around the bedspread like the beam of a lighthouse trawling the face of the ocean. She's agitated for a minute but it's OK. She sees her wedding album. Her little life raft of survivors sailing on the bedspread. Everything is alright again. She must have turned off the light automatically and fallen asleep. But now she's back.

And Hughie is back. She finds his photograph. Outside a pub with a low thatched roof somewhere in Limerick. Tea. Yes. They had tea there. Birdie can see the jester in him now. The fool he plays. The way he slopes himself against the wall and looks out to one side, ignoring the camera. And all the bicycles lined up against the wall. Those were the days. She turns over the photo and reads the faded writing.

– Don't try to teach a pig to sing. You won't succeed. And you'll annoy the pig! –

It makes her laugh. Even now in the deepest darkness of the night. She props him up against the base of the bedside lamp. The cheeky devil. 'I have my eye on you,' she whispers at the picture. 'I have my eye on you, Mr Dattledo Donoghue!'

Nine months after the honeymoon Augustine Delaney was born, named after a grandfather of the same name, and who, like many Cork people of the nineteenth century, had a high regard for the Augustinian Friars in that city. There were jokes, of course, among the travelling salesmen but nobody took offence. Alex would go into Mannion's Bar in the evenings to buy six bottles of stout, which he took home wrapped in a brown paper bag and Hughie would stick his head out from behind the fogged glass of the snug. 'How's our child?' Hughie would inquire, and the travelling salesmen would fall about the place laughing, because Hughie had told them the story of how he had shared the Vet's honeymoon with the wife. It never bothered Birdie. No. Nor Alex.

And when they got as far as Kerry, it was Birdie who insisted that they couldn't under any circumstances abandon him so far from home. She wouldn't dream of letting him go. Not in Kerry. For goodness sake they couldn't have half the fun if he wasn't there, with his flute, impressing all the musicians from Kerry with his furious tunes.

They had fun. That's the only word for it. Fun on the road. Innocent fun. All three of them. For four amazing days. And then it was over.

It was all over. They returned to Ballinasloe in silence and waved goodbye to Hughie at Mannion's corner.

And as the Skehana people say, there's more to life than romance. That's something Birdie found out for certain. Seeing the Vet's cream long johns on the kitchen floor for the tenth time when she was sorting the laundry. That was a turning point. Hearing him fart in the bedroom. That was a milestone. Cleaning his beard hair from the sink hole. But it was called marriage. It was called being Mrs Delaney. She knew that there was going to be more to marriage than what you saw in American films, and even in those some of the women didn't come out so good. But she didn't mind. In fact, she considered herself the luckiest woman in Ireland to wait hand and foot on Alex Delaney. And besides, Daddy had moved to the County Home where he could do no harm other than to stare at the ceiling and wait patiently to die, so there were certain things to be thankful for in every situation.

And then suddenly Alex farts so loudly that she wakes up again. Jesus, Mary and Joseph, she shouts, who farted? But it wasn't Alex. Because she was just asleep again and now she's so shocked with the sound of the fart, it was so distinct, and so huge, that she sits up in the bed, her reading glasses like a tractor's headlamps, and she looks at the night in Killarney, and the trip around the lake in the jaunting cart, and the walk on the long beach on the last morning, and she feels enormous gratitude. And Hughie's sad eyes light up every photograph that they took with the new little Kodak camera Alex had bought as a gift for her on the way through Limerick.

Hughie navigated the pair of them up roads and down byways they would never have found on their own. They heard music played by women on little concertinas, and by men on fiddles, which would have made the angels weep.

'Would make the angels weep,' Hughie said. 'The way I like it. Slow and sorrowful.'

And in those days Hughie was still full of boyish fun. He was only thirty. People said he had his own love affair tucked away somewhere in the forests of Cong. And he certainly had the aura of experience. The scent of a dog that enjoys being off the porch at regular intervals. He would sit beside the ladies and put his long fingers on the buttons of their concertinas to take a little jig out of it and sometimes he'd whisper scatological crudities in their ears.

An old-fashioned man. He believed in courting women and flirting with them, and he displayed an enthusiasm for their company that far outstripped his interest in music.

No matter what room he walked into, women instantly trusted him with their lives. He was that class of a man.

And thank God she has her photographs for if she didn't

have them, she wonders would she remember anything. And then she'd be daft. And they could put her away.

And in those days women were rarely seen in the bars, though it seemed an exception was made for musicians, who invariably drank ginger ale or tonic wine, or glasses of stout with spoons of sugar stirred in.

Birdie glowed in her blue stewardess costume and could be coerced into a few Babychams while the Vet leaned in on the bar, taking whiskey with the Kerry farmers, and Hughie played jigs with the ladies, and nodded over his flute to indicate the end of 'Drowsy Maggie'.

She was more than happy with Hughie. She encouraged him. He would cross the galaxy just to be in the company of a woman. Wasn't that the kind of man anyone wanted?

And the women often asked Hughie would he not settle down. Ah for Jaysus sake! Settle down! Sure men like Dattledo don't settle down.

'Would you not settle down, Dattledo?'

Hughie's body stretched like a wild cat and he purred into her ear that he hadn't found the right woman. Or that he was too hard to please. Oh he could send volts of terror through the spines of his young admirers. She used to ask him just for fun. Just to hear him purr.

'Would you not settle down there, Dattledo?'

But isn't it funny too, how things change. A few years after Gussie was born, Hughie and the Vet drifted apart.

There was no reason. Maybe Hughie's nomadic lifestyle seemed at odds with the domestic responsibilities of fatherhood. It might not have been anything in particular. And they always remained friends. She knew that. There was no falling out or anything like that. But marriage defined a new universe for Alex. And they said that Hughie went bitter. Something happened inside him. Something that forced him down like a plane. Like a bird shot out of the air. Something. Couldn't be named. Maybe it was nothing. Just in him. Like we all have a life mapped out for us in our bones before we're born.

And then Birdie wonders is there someone at the foot of the bed. She senses something. A presence. No more substantial than the shadow of the wardrobe falling on the wall, but it speaks, and Birdie would know Alex's voice anywhere.

'Hughie descended into hell,' the shadow declares with great authority. And the voice is slightly stilted, like Dracula's. 'Hughie descended into hell,' the shadow repeats, 'where only the drink can compensate for the unbearable passing of time and the lost opportunities.'

That certainly woke her.

3

AND JUST HOLD ON a minute. She's in the bed. And the wedding album is on the floor. It had slid off the bedcover. The photographs are scattered all over the duvet. OK. But who cares? It's the wrong album.

That's not the album she wants at all. Is it? No. And those are not the photographs she needs. Not tonight. That's why she keeps waking. She's been looking at the wrong pictures.

Firstly there was the leather photo album downstairs. And then there was the wedding album in the wardrobe. But there was a third option. Wasn't there?

Slowly easing herself up off the bed, she moves around the room to the wardrobe. She replaces the photos in the back cover of the wedding album, and then folds the tissue paper around it before settling it back into the box. Her back is cold. She must be careful of that. The heating is not on and the night is freezing. She shouldn't be standing around in her nightdress.

But where are the other photographs? Where is her life? She gets a sudden rush of panic. Where? It's always the same. Like when she mislays her keys. The fear that someone has stolen them. It's just that she can't remember for a moment. Her mind goes away for a few seconds. And then it comes back. 'Thank God,' she whispers, when it returns. She closes the wardrobe. Unlocks her bedroom door. Shuffles out onto the landing.

Birdie is no fool. No. And there's no danger of her falling down the stairs if she sticks to the rules. So once again she sits on the top step and then moves down one at a time. Feet first. Then bum. Until she's at the bottom. That's an achievement at this hour of the night.

Now where are they? Under the stairs? Yes. She flicks on the light. Pushes back the rack of coats. Peers in at the shelf behind the coats. The shoe polish. OK. Brushes. Yes. Studded golfing shoes. The top of the old wooden driver. A box of golf balls. What looks like a brush, except the teeth are as hard as nails. She stares at that; wonders what it's for.

Hush Puppies! That's what it's for. Yes. Hush Puppies.

The Vet wore Hush Puppies in his retirement, because of the bunion.

And there they are at last. Tiny little photos, squashed into a red tin box with the word Oxo on the lid, and hidden at the back of the shelf. She reaches for the box. She knows before she opens it that they are inside. Her treasure.

She returns to the stairs and sits on the first step and hugs the little red tin. Now she can really open everything. Because everything is in the box.

On Friday afternoons, when Gussie was little and not yet a scholar with the nuns, he would sit on the back seat of Birdie's Raleigh bicycle, and they would freewheel down the avenue and out the gate and farther down the hilly road towards town. In those days there were hardly any houses on the long mile stretch between home and the little stone bridge over the river, which marked the beginning of what they called 'the main road'. Old Mrs McWeeney, a woman who wore black clothes and had white hair, lived in a musty drawing room in a grand two-storey nineteenth-century mansion with bay windows. The walls were built of grey slate stone that looked like the sky on a rainy day. And farther down the hill were the two Misses Bewleys, spinsters who lived in a more modest farmhouse without character.

Neither the Misses Bewleys nor Mrs McWeeney were ever seen. Their families had hunted the fox with horses and hounds, and owned all the land in the vicinity of the town. In the new Irish Republic they had little inclination to engage in local society, apart from selling their assets like slices of ham to the local building contractor. Birdie used their mysterious and invisible presence as a weapon to frighten Gussie. If ever he refused to eat his cabbage or turned over the coffee table in a tantrum, or knocked the head off the Child of Prague, which he did one day with a pillow, she'd threaten to deliver him to Mrs McWeeney.

'She knows how to look after children who don't behave themselves,' Birdie would say. It always worked. Every Friday, on their way into town on the bike, Birdie would invite him to turn his head sideways as they passed the gates to see if Mrs McWeeney was at her window.

She was always there. The bottom half of the lace curtain pulled back by a hand floating in the darkness. The vague outline of a white head farther back in the dark room. It made him shiver. And worse were the windows of the Bewleys' house, from which, he supposed, light never emerged. Gussie would not even dare to look in the direction of those windows, for in that darkness he feared he might see too much.

But most shocking of all was when the tinkers arrived. The gypsies with their roll-top wagons. Their piebald horses and ragged donkeys camped beside the stone bridge. They camped just off the main road, beside the gorse bushes, which they festooned with their drying underwear. They had mad dogs chained to the wheels of the wagons, and mucky-faced children stood at the blackened stones of a previous night's fire, their backsides bare to the wind.

I'll leave you there, Birdie would say, if you're not good.

Poor Gussie. Did she frighten him too much? He'd wrap his little hands around the springs under the saddle and hold on for dear life. The poor wee rabbit. But Birdie wasn't thinking much of rabbits then. She was thinking of lamb chops and roast beef and how well she looked on her bicycle, with her chest pushed out like a pigeon on the gate.

It's so easy now to look back and admit that she was stuck up. To admit that she was too full of herself living in her splendidly detached mansion, with a perfect child on the back of the bike as she wheeled it into town to rub everyone's noses in the triumphs they all thought she'd never achieve. And even then, she was fooling nobody only herself. Put a beggar on horseback, they said, and she would ride to hell. Whoosh! Whoosh! That's how her life went betimes. In a whoosh!

Now it's all in a little tin box as she sits at the foot of the stairs and just as she opens it, she hears the whoosh again. Whoosh!

She'd call to the butcher and the baker and the vegetable stall on the street, and she'd order what she required, and pay them, and then later that evening, or maybe the following morning, the messenger boys would bring it all out to her back door. The messenger boys on their bicycles, with box-baskets strapped onto the front handlebars, pushing their way up the avenue, and whistling through their teeth and standing every few seconds to comb the Brylcreem into their black waves of hair.

In town Birdie would indulge herself in a venomous bout of complaining and whingeing. As if it was a burden to be well-heeled. She'd go on moaning relentlessly about the house. About the size of it. It was too big. And too far out of town. And she had to cycle the lonely road every Friday to do the messages. Wasn't that terrible? And Gussie on the carrier! And if the road wasn't lonely, then it was too busy, with all them tinkers, and you wouldn't like to be caught in crossfire with a pair of them latchicos on your way home. Oh now, there was nothing but trouble. And so many rooms in the new house. Well, you wouldn't believe it. Impossible it was to keep them all clean for his lordship. Who? Alex. Mr Delaney. The Vet! Oh, of course.

But no one gave her any encouragement. Men in brown shop coats with smiles like lacquered doors stood silent until she finished.

'Oh give me the Earl Grey! Mr Delaney doesn't like the cheap tea.'

Down Main Street she scooted with defiant glee. Past the terraces where her childhood friends were boiling pots of crude greasy stew and skivvying for battalions of children and useless husbands, or past drapery shops where some of them were still serving behind the counter and facing the joyless destiny of middle age in spinster corsets. And them were the ones that said she'd never get a ring on her finger! The ones who said her tits were too withered to suckle a child! That's what they said all right. And by Jesus, sometimes she pedalled as furious as a spider climbing up out of the bath and she'd say, by Jesus I'll cut the fucken socks off them today.

She grew a forest of enemies. And drew occasional fire from shopkeepers and friends who were sick to the back teeth of Birdie and her perfect life.

Alex was a man who wore strong aftershave, white shoes, pressed cream or grey suits, and bright yellow ties. Her enemies didn't need great imaginations to concoct the most exotic of scenarios for that costume.

What was he doing in Cork? they wanted to know. As if the southern city might be a place like Sodom or Gomorrah. And why did he leave it? And how come a man so apparently gifted in the arts of husbandry should have left it so late in life to find a mate? Did she ever think of that?

No one ever went as close to the bone as Betty Burke. An explicit charge. Told Birdie to her face that Alex spent more time in the golf club with the pretty young boys from the secondary college than he did with Birdie, whose visits to the same club were limited to humiliating hours sitting in the ladies' tea room, in a lambswool white dress, with white pearls, a soft, feathery white hat the size of a saucer on her head, and nobody to talk to, while Alex loitered around the bar until well past midnight. Loitered! Betty's word.

Only gentlemen were allowed in the golf-club bar at that time, where the best sport was to argue with the teenagers from the local secondary school who had been caddying all day, and had been seduced into staying for a few minerals with their elders and betters: the overfed professional classes who squashed the boys like sardines into accidental corners and breathed stale smoky whiskey breath on them like dragons full of unconscious desires.

On festive occasions, such as the Captain's Prize or the President's Day, the ladies amused themselves in the tea room, an adjoining long hall with a dance floor surrounded by little wooden tables and chairs. And if the men didn't join the ladies by nine o'clock, they were considered to have overstepped the boundary of provincial discretion.

What Betty Burke referred to was a night the previous year when Alex had been in the bar until after midnight, and Birdie had to hang onto the Burkes for the entire evening, her neck stretched in humiliation, like a dying swan without its mate.

But Birdie was loyal.

'That,' she told Betty, 'is because Alex is educated. He likes talking to the college boys, because the rest of the crowd in the golf links are only fucken ignoramuses.'

'Now, now,' says Betty, 'don't use that language in my shop. That language may be alright in the terraces, but we don't use it in this establishment.'

'They're still fucken ignoramuses. No matter what language they use.'

This time the punch had landed.

'My Tommy,' Betty whispered, 'is no fucken ignoramus!' The smile still holding on to her white talcumed face like a sheet in a storm, an Afton cigarette still clinging to the lipstick in the side of her mouth.

'Well, he never went to college,' Birdie declared.

'Neither did you, Miss Waters.'

'I didn't have to,' says Birdie, and she flew out the door, onto her bike, and belted down the street, in triumph maybe, or rage, or just confusion, and Gussie sitting on the carrier and holding on to the saddle for dear life and crying 'Mammy, Mammy, you're going too fast.'

'Whoosh!' she said to Gussie. Whoosh! And it's as if someone clicked their fingers and she's sitting on the bottom step of the stairs holding an Oxo box.

Whoosh!

4

NO WORDS CAN SAY how much she loved the Vet. How much she opened her heart and shared all the little secrets and worries of her life with him. And indeed he listened carefully to everything she said. She knew this for certain, because not long after her altercation with Betty Burke, and in that very same golf club one night, Alex Delaney faced a crucial test. Birdie was about to discover exactly what class of man she had married.

There was a long counter at the far end of the tea room. It was stacked high with sandwiches, pastries, jam rolls, meringue buns, fresh fruit salad, mince pies, strudels, pancakes, flans of peach and pear, and bowls of cream, jellies, custards, and a pan of tiramisu that the architect's wife had baked from a recipe she had been sent from her sister who was married to an Englishman and lived in Greece. The tiramisu was the jewel in the crown.

It was mayhem around the counter. Ladies coming and going, setting plates, arranging displays, settling the flowers, removing someone's handbag. It was an extravaganza of colour and texture. A single montage of crinoline, silk and nylon in heaps of blue and cream and pastel pink where all the pretty ladies sat at the top table, beside the food counter, in their frocks of billowy bouffant, lavishly trimmed in lace, and nylon parchment underskirts with ribbon rushing, and soft nylon tricot bodices with more lace trimming, inside swanky jackets with big lapels and giant buttons, and the daring Mrs Edmonton in her black trouser suit, and the older ladies in dark black silk, and crimson red shawls, with chunky chains of gold hanging around their necks.

Birdie was adorned in white mohair wool, with a little tiara of white feathers, like a small child at her First Holy Communion. She was nervous and shy. She had brought an offering of little coconut cakes and simple buns made with egg and flour and a tiny bit of jam in the centre of each. Tiramisu was overdoing it a bit, Birdie thought. And the architect's wife looked like a baked cadaver after wasting all that money on a holiday with her sister.

Birdie had no one to talk with, so she clung to Betty Burke and her cronies at the top table, which wasn't so comfortable after their recent exchange of fire. The ladies were busy hiding away the best tarts and pastries in the kitchen, or at the back of the display, so that when the night was over they could slip the stash into the boots of their cars and feast on them with their families for the rest of the week.

Betty Burke's gang was known as 'the top brass'. Women

with good heels and old money. From landed families who paid the piper long before the foundations had been dug for the little galvanized pavilion that constituted the new golf club in 1934. Convent girls reared only to provide homes for the small coterie of professional men in the town. Ladies who ran the town by shaping opinion, telling the priests what to say and what to do, and by sticking together like glue at social gatherings.

Standing before that battalion of style in the tea room, and holding her little coconut cakes on a wicker tray, Birdie wished that Alex was beside her. He was the man who could chat to the ladies. And she could talk to him. In fact he was the only one she really did talk to since her wedding day. The only person she opened her heart to. But she was alone in the crowd for almost an hour.

When he did come into the tea room a few minutes after nine, and saw her sitting alone, he went over to her immediately and put his arm around her, and it might be expected that he would stay there. That's what Birdie hoped. But on the other hand there were no other men yet in the room. And Birdie could well understand his dilemma. He didn't want to leave her there on her own. But neither could he just sit like a pharaoh in a milk tub of virgins. It would look stupid. It wasn't time for the men to come in yet. There were too many frocks and not enough suits.

So he asked her would she mind if he was just another little minute in the bar because one of the young boys from the college was very interested in doing veterinary science at university, and Alex felt obliged to offer him extended advice on the matter. And Birdie said, of course. But she was nervous. He must have seen that. She was in pain. Sitting there alone, with her white, feathery little cap and not a single bitch with the decency to bid her the time of day as they fluttered around their flans and meringues.

Alex marched out again and Birdie could see the ladies nodding knowingly to each other as if to say, yes, there he goes, we won't be seeing him again until two in the morning.

But they got it wrong. The fucken bitches. They got it wrong.

The top brass had kept themselves cheerful from about seven until ten, by dressing and redressing the tables. Hiding apple tarts and whipping cream. Then they set out the prizes for the prize-giving. That moved things on a bit. The silver cups. The cut-glass goblets. The bone china. By ten o'clock there were trays of alcohol floating discreetly through the hatch between the bar and the tea room with alarming speed. Their nerves were frayed. It was the moment of truth when the herd came from the bar. Every woman prayed that her man would be present and correct. Not pissed or missing.

The first surprise was a tray of gin and tonics for Betty and her mates. It floated down the hall in the hands of a good-looking lanky boy with long black hair, who said he was Doctor Bradley's son. That got the ladies swooning. The boy said the drinks were with the compliments of the Vet. Score one.

Then the bell tinkled for the speeches and the gentlemen appeared, red-eyed, good-humoured, and bristling for the prize-giving. Alex was the first in the door. He sat beside Birdie and put his arm around her again, in what the top brass considered to be an unnecessary gesture of intimacy.

Though it was no surprise to anyone when it was announced that Alex had hit the best score of the day and was asked to step forward to receive the Captain's Prize.

He said a few words about being no good at golf, but he supposed that there were no prizes for the things he was good at. Ladies put their hands to their mouths in measured displays of shock, while the men at the back cheered and everyone declared that truly the best man had won.

The three-piece band struck up a samba. Alex swept up his beloved Birdie, whose dainty steps followed him around the room like a robin hopping after a blackbird. They swept the boards, gliding with rigour and triumph, and doing what they loved to do best. They danced.

Is that why he had married her? they wondered. Simply that! She could dance. They danced around the room on their own. They were so good that it took ages before a second couple had the courage to join them. They were a spectacle. Foxtrot, waltz or samba, they did it, like Fred and Ginger, and you either admired them or hated their guts. But make no mistake, they could dance. And when the saxophone blew the last note, they ended up right in front of Betty Burke's table. Her Sweet Afton floating in the air beside her white powdered face.

'Are you not dancing, Elizabeth?' he inquired with the grace of a crocodile talking to its dinner. Her rich red lips parted in a smile as pleasant as if her bowels were being clawed out personally by Birdie.

'Ah shure you know yourself, Alex,' says she, 'my Tommy was born with two left feet.'

Some of the other ladies said that the Vet was far too generous buying everybody drink, and they invited Birdie to sit down, and then Betty and Birdie nattered away for the rest of the night like two long-lost friends and they forgot about the mother and father of an argument they had

had just two weeks earlier, and Birdie knew she was in. She had joined the top brass.

It was great fun after that. Except Betty smoked too much. At regular intervals she had to cough her way to and from the toilet like a cow with TB.

The men lined up to ask Birdie for a dance. Doctor Bradley and the Engineer and even the Reverend Richardson. They all wanted to dance with a woman as light on her feet as Birdie. Even younger men, trying to find their way up in the social world where Alex was the star, spent the night watching for their chance with Birdie.

What a life! And such fun! Dancing the night away. Not a worry in the world. Proud as a goose in the farmyard, waddling around behind her gander.

Birdie could tell him everything. And yet she could tell him nothing. When she had an altercation with the butcher or the baker, or one of her friends, she could give a blow-by-blow account, and Alex would stand at the hearth in the dining room, his backside to the fire, a bottle of stout in one hand and a cigarette in the other. He'd laugh.

That's what she remembers about him. Because it's difficult at such a distance to remember anything about him. Sometimes he fades completely. Sometimes he comes back like a shadow. Like a voice. And finally he's there. But the laugh was the thing. That's how you'd know him in a dark room.

She had pleaded with him to stop drinking in town. And he agreed. He made a compromise. He brought the bags of stout home and uncorked them in the dining room and relaxed as well as if he was in the snug in Mannion's.

He'd tell her all his little adventures. Everything that had happened since morning on the highways and byways of the country, as he went around attending to sick animals and their daft owners. He was fond of saying that in four out of five cases, a vet finds that the animal is in perfect health, whereas the farmer is completely mad.

Birdie doesn't remember what he looked like. That is the worst thing about life as a widow. Not to be allowed say that she can't remember what he looked like. That she sometimes forgets even the sound of his laughter or what kind of eyes he had. And sometimes she can't even recognize him in the old photos.

The day she had the row with Betty, she told the whole thing to Alex the minute he came home. She told him almost everything. But she left out the last bit.

The last bit was when she was strapping Gussie into the carrier seat of her bicycle and Betty came to the door, holding the doorpost with her hand as if she might not have the breath to stand, and she cursed her. That's what it felt like.

'Go home now to your house, Bernie Waters, and dust your old fancy furniture, for maybe it's all you'll have at the end of the day. For you sure and certain won't have many friends in this town.'

That's not a very nice thing for Birdie to remember when she's rummaging under the stairs, and wondering what she's doing there, and racking her brains to remember what she might be looking for alone in the middle of the night, lost in the coats, and then sitting on the steps of the stairs wondering – what the hell did I come down for?

Not knowing. Not knowing. Not knowing. Even when the little Oxo box is sitting on her lap and staring her in the face. Still not knowing. OK, she came down for the Oxo box. But why? What did she want that for? She can't remember.

That's the curse you see. What Betty said wounded her.

84

And she put it away with all the other hurtful things gathered up during a lifetime. Like a magpie, she stores things in her heart. Nurtures them and takes them out and goes over them again and again. It's like counting spoons in a drawer.

Birdie always does her counting in the middle of the night, or very early in the morning when she can't sleep.

She makes a great collection of sayings that have wounded her over the years. She can't remember her husband's face sometimes. But she can remember the wounds. The wounds that shaped her.

What about the porridge? That's a good idea. A sudden idea. Into the kitchen she goes and puts the flakes in a bowl and then pours a cup of cold water over that and finally places the bowl in the microwave. It's simple.

No pots. No fuss.

But she has just done it when she immediately forgets it. Doesn't know where the bowl is. Can't remember where she put it two seconds ago. She wants to scream at someone. Where's my porridge? She searches for a pot.

But nothing to be found. They're all clean. Where's the porridge?

And a moment later she finds it again. She's been making it in the microwave for years. It had just slipped her mind for a second. But that's the way her mind works now. There are little gaps. Where nothing exists. And nothing, not even the names in her own little prayer book can be recalled. Until the tide comes in again, and the electricity goes back on, and she is able to continue with her breakfast, even though it's three o'clock in the morning.

The Oxo box is on the kitchen table. How did it get there? Perhaps there is something important in it. She wouldn't have come downstairs for no reason. No.

She takes it in her arms and sits down and places it on her knees, and she thinks one sudden thought. A cup of tea. That's a good idea. Make a cup of tea.

5

NO ONE COULD DENY that Birdie kept a clean house. She always did. Warm and full of food. The Vet ached with happiness when he crossed the threshold. Birdie was always making dumplings for her little bunny, as she called Gussie, because when he was frightened, his big brown eyes opened very wide and he became still and he reminded her of a rabbit caught in the headlamps of the Vet's Austin. And Gussie often slept with her. Snuggling into her back for warmth when he had a nightmare. He clung to her on the back of the bike as she pedalled into town to do battle with the spinsters of Ballinasloe.

He is still clinging to her. Even in the kitchen, at this time of night. Even though he's dead. In his coffin. Even though he is as cold as a stone in the ditch. Even though all is quiet in the sanctuary of the church at this very moment. He still stares down at her from his graduation photograph on the kitchen wall. The black gown around his shoulders, and the scroll of paper resting in his hands. His eyes wide with achievement and pride.

He was always clinging to her. Even when she wasn't in the house, he'd sit in the wardrobe and play with her shoes and sniff at her frocks. And he'd make tiny bouquets for her from the flowers in the front garden and he'd leave them on the hall table until he saw her shadow in the glass of the front door and then he'd rush to her with his whole heart.

When she became pregnant with him, everyone agreed she had a lot of courage to face childbirth at her age. She would have said she hadn't a lot of choice in the matter. Courage didn't come into it. But sure enough her blood pressure jumped through the roof the day she went into hospital for the tests. Nobody could explain the chart, so they sent her to Galway in an ambulance. The siren gave her a headache.

And by the time she got there the blood pressure was normal again. She returned to Ballinasloe the following day. 'Welcome back, Mrs Delaney. Were you on your holidays? Will we check the blood pressure now?' And guess what! It was back up through the roof. Wasn't that odd?

Back to Galway. Such a merry-go-round. But this time they kept her. Said they might have to keep her there for the duration of the pregnancy, which caused a right flutter in the golf club. The Vet was terrified. He ate his dinners in Hayden's Hotel and spent the nights hugging pints in Mannion's Bar. The other clients asked in sombre tones if there was any news. They looked as if it was already a foregone conclusion that Birdie would be buried in a wedding dress, with the little dead baby folded in her arms. All because of a little bit of blood pressure. Sure it was way out of all proportion!

She remained in Galway for six weeks, being monitored twenty-four hours a day, though her blood pressure stayed normal all that time, and her heartbeat was normal, and every bloody thing about the pregnancy was going according to the laws of nature. Eventually they released her. Alex wheeled her to the door with a pink hospital blanket around her waist, and gently manoeuvred her into the rear passenger seat of the station wagon. And he had tears in his eyes as he drove her home. She could see them in the rear-view mirror.

'Do you know something, Birdie?' he said. 'I thought you were going to leave me.'

She just looked out the window and smiled. She didn't tell him everything.

She didn't tell him it was the nun. She didn't tell him that when she went for her first check up, the old nun was waiting for her. A straight-boned nun with a white face and white hair and a white habit. A nun so white and cold in her gaze that even the doctors were afraid of her. She was the one who had pushed Birdie's blood pressure through the roof. Sister Bernard had told her to take down her drawers and lie on the cold steel slab, and then she had taken her own two saintly hands, that Birdie always thought were meant for sewing shrouds in the convent or pressing wafers together for the Holy Communion of the Mass, and she had stuck them, without a by-your-leave, up the sweet and secret darkness that Birdie had thought was the exclusive preserve of her lovely Vet. Sister Bernard had it all done in a jiffy. To check that everything was where it should be, as she said. She had an expression of distaste on her face, carrying centuries of theology in every sweet and condescending grimace.

But it wasn't the examination alone that raised the blood pressure in Birdie's palpitating heart muscle, and which could be clearly seen through her cotton vest, beating its rage like a lamb's neck in the slaughterhouse. It wasn't that alone. It was the hurtful things the old nun had said to her. Those were the things she never told anyone. Not even the Vet. Those were things Birdie would keep in her heart for centuries, if she had to.

Those are the things that come out now, in the dead of

the night, as Gussie smiles down from the wall and she sits in the kitchen with a mug of tea beside her Oxo box on the table. It's the Oxo box that upsets her. It always did. The Oxo box that smells of nun.

6

EVERYBODY WAS THERE. Everybody saw it. When the Vet slipped into her arms for the first time, at a half-crown dance in the local town hall.

The doctor's daughter was there. And the daughters of three solicitors. It was a beautiful array. An enormous amount of young girls. All lined up along the wall like flowers on the altar. Perfumed as sweetly as princesses. The Comerford twins, picking their noses. The sergeant's big girl. And the five daughters of the man who owned half the shops on Main Street. A flock. A convent. A gaggle.

And so beautiful, in contrast to the pack of yahoos and gimps huddled inside the door. The guttersnipes on the balcony. The teddy boys at the mouth of the men's toilets, combing their greasy manes. What Betty Burke called the dregs of society. Boys who usually went to the one-shilling hops. Boys who would climb in the toilet windows to get a gawk at dressed-up rich girls. At the hundreds of legs in sheer nylon, the princesses in crinoline, the lips sparkling like sweat on a raspberry. Moist hands clinging to tiny black or white handbags that were all the rage at that time.

Some of the girls wore long-sleeved white gloves that went all the way up to their oxters, to hide the sweat. And others had slim cigarette cases of pure silver. Everyone dreaming of the moment they might sit in the Vet's car on the road home. Dreaming of that American moment. That film thing. Yes. There was more to cigarettes than was on the packet.

There weren't a lot of vets in Ballinasloe. Nor were there many of those teddy boys who could afford to be driving around in a spotless black Ford, like Mr Delaney. And though every single girl on the floor was desperate for a good man, Birdie knew that only *she* had a chance. As sure as there were eyes in her head, she could say for certain that not a one of them virgins could dance a foxtrot.

Birdie read the situation the instant she looked down onto the dance floor. She was on the balcony. She could sense the breath leaving her body with fright. She thought she was about to faint. Christ, it was such a shock. She tried to look again, to make sure she could believe her eyes. She surveyed them carefully. The entire line of virgins, alleged virgins and hopeless spinsters in the hall below.

Delaney was on the floor. She saw him glide. Turn. Reverse. Samba. She saw him samba. Christ, he could dance. The style of it! And all they could do was giggle and trample on his toes. The poor man!

That's why she went down immediately, as the committee began serving the tea. She marched across the floor, making a beeline for him, quick as she could, before the Dinny Hughes Big Band dared announce a Lady's Choice. A Lady's Choice would have ruined her. She stood before the Vet and stuck out her hand and introduced herself.

No trimmings required.

'How do you do? I'm Birdie Waters. Are you the new vet?'

He confessed that he was indeed the new man in town.

'I see you can dance,' says she. Not a compliment, mind

you. No. An evaluation. A statement of measure.

'The neck of her.' She heard them. But let them call her what they like. Birdie knew that none of them was a match for her.

That was it. The Vet took her hand in his hand, and placed the palm of his right hand between her shoulder blades, and off they went. She could glide across that floor with such ease that he realized she was a treasure from the word go. The rest of them didn't have a look in, once she got him on his feet for the first time.

And in the years that followed there was something else he treasured more than her little feet, and that was her honesty. She spoke her mind. She told him all her secrets, and she demanded his.

As she walked across the floor of the town hall that night, and stuck her hand out, some of the snooty bitches could be heard bemoaning the recently abandoned social practice of class segregation. Half-crown dances used to be reserved strictly for the well-heeled, and shilling hops for the children of the poor.

There was a time, and it wasn't that long ago, they muttered, when teddy boys didn't get in toilet windows, and girls from the terraces would have more self-respect than to march up to a member of the professional classes and force him to dance.

But there was no sign on Alex Delaney's face that he had been forced into anything. In fact he looked the picture of contentment as he glided around, spinning her, turning her, in ever more extravagant flourishes and twirls as the evening progressed. Every sign on his face that the woman he had been waiting for had just entered his life.

7

SHE CAN'T BEAR looking at that Oxo box. Why is it sitting there? And who took it out? Birdie needs to sleep. She needs to sleep. She has a long day to get through. The darkest of all days. So she leaves the kitchen and holds the wall as she moves down the hall, and then up the stairs. Slowly now. One step at a time. One hand on the banister. One hand on the wall. That's it. That's good. And back to her room again. Pull back the bedspread and the blankets for the umpteenth time. Ease herself down onto the pillow. Must sleep. Must be ready for the morning. Christ help her to sleep.

And He does. Christ, indeed, helps in a kind of a way.

Because that's when she begins to hear the organ playing.

Oh that's lovely! That's a relief! That's a good sign. The organ is a good sign.

She hears it often as she lies in bed. After sleepless nights when she has been tortured by the things she told nobody in a lifetime. Bombarded by hurtful things her memory stored up over the decades. Sometimes she reaches dawn in a lather of sweat, breathless and exhausted from the struggle. But she is always relieved when the music returns.

And with the first light of day now filtering through the curtain, she begins to hear the organ, playing again, as she floats in a bed that has been the safest and most beautiful place in the world she has ever known.

It's the bed the Vet bought in a furniture store in Athlone. And she complained at the time. Protested. Said it was too much money. But he wouldn't hear of it. He kept saying it was worth every penny. And maybe she was inclined to agree, the day the lorry arrived from Athlone, causing a stir behind the lace-curtained windows on the main street as it

92

drove through town with that big bed sticking out of the rear end. The delivery lorry processed slowly up the avenue to the Vet's hall door. Birdie stood there with a dishcloth in her hand. In those days she was rarely seen answering the front door without a dishcloth in her hand.

Her heart was palpitating. A mixture of excitement and fear.

First off the lorry were the table and four chairs for the dining room. Then a dark mahogany sideboard. They were impressive. But it was the carved lattices and curves of the bed boards, and the sheer size of the Odearest mattress that gave Birdie goosebumps. She had to sit down on one of the chairs in a fluster of anxiety, as the two men with Roscommon accents, assisted by the Vet and his one-time boarding house companion Eugene Devine, negotiated the bed and mattress in the door and up the stairs. Assembled it in that very room where it has lasted, just as the glossy magazine had promised, for a lifetime.

Eugene Devine was small, bald and pot-bellied, and he had fat little fingers, and he had to stretch his feet to hit the organ pedals, and nobody ever believed he was an organist, until they heard the bellows roar. Eugene, like a commander-in-chief, making great emotions burst forth from the pipes in the organ loft with the squeeze of his plump little fingers. That was Eugene. And then the church fashions changed, and the organ fell silent, and Eugene went off down a labyrinth of the town's little side streets walking his dog for an unbearable amount of years.

Then the dog disappeared, and Eugene continued for a while, with sunken red eyes that constantly streamed water, and required him to hold a white handkerchief in his left hand forever.

Eventually Eugene disappeared. He was a bachelor. Nobody knew what illness he had been suffering from for years, apart from the nurses who changed his dressings once a week.

But he's still there with Birdie. And in the last hours before dawn she can walk through her desolate house and still hear the plaintive music that Eugene's little fingers commanded out of thin air. Not the thunder of 'Here Comes the Bride'. No. That was Eugene's pièce de résistance, which he had let rip in the church at the end of every wedding, for as long as anyone could remember. He called it 'World War Three'.

But that's not what Birdie hears. She hears the soft whisper of the harmonium playing Gounod's 'Ave Maria', as Eugene played it on that September morning in a small church on a hill just outside the town. It was a gothic stone church, flanked by two grand chestnuts. It was so small. And she loved the shafts of amber light that filtered through the stained glass behind the altar, and the smell of candle grease. It was like being at the door of heaven, the old people used to say.

Not to put a tooth in it, she was delighted that the canon, the old sourpuss, had refused to marry her in the main church in the middle of town.

The Vet had been talking about a friend of his, a priest out in Africa who was coming home, whom he hoped might officiate at the wedding. Well, the canon nearly had apoplexy. A dour old cleric, with folds of flesh falling off the bones on the side of his face, which gave him a disturbing resemblance to the gundog that snored on the rug beside the fire. Oh but the holy cleric was indignant that he, as parish priest, as canon up on his horse, would not be considered adequate to the task of marrying one of his own parishioners. Particularly, says he, particularly, that woman. But the Vet wasn't a man to cower before the clergy. No, sir. And so they found a compromise, which adequately hurt both of them. The couple could have their guest priest if they wanted, but they couldn't have the main church in the town.

And so it happened. As the chestnut trees outside the door showed signs of golden rust on the frayed edges of their leaves, and the first ripe chestnuts could be seen, as shiny as the flank of a horse, inside the opening pods on the cement paving, Birdie's father walked her to the door. Waited there. And Eugene pumped the harmonium with his little feet, like a child pedalling a bike up a hill. For a few seconds the congregation could only hear the organist grunting, and then finally the first notes of 'Ave Maria' wheezed out of the old instrument.

Birdie never stopped loving that church, never stopped being drawn to it. She buried the Vet there behind the church twenty-six years later. And she never missed the annual visitation to the graves each November. No matter how difficult it was. No matter that she had to walk from the car, or stand in the wind, or look down at the little blue plastic bucket of flowers that she propped against the headstone, to declare that after all those years she was still as attentive as on the day of her wedding to a man the town knew nothing about.

A man who died from carelessness and neglect. No point in glossing over the facts. Birdie called a spade a spade when she needed to. Alex went into hospital with a slight pain in his left hip. But by the time they were finished poking him, and testing him, and making a dog's dinner of lumbar punctures, his body was so exhausted that they moved him to the County Home where he got bedsores the size of golf balls on his hips and died the year after.

She sat at his side every day until the end. And she brought him tea and home-made buns because they had shared buns and tea from the moment they had met on the dancehall floor. And he always loved the cup of tea. He'd raise it in the air and say it was the cup that cheered but did not inebriate. And on the day he died she gave him the tea, and a coconut bun, and he enjoyed them both. He patted her head as he often did and he said, 'Oh, Birdie, you're a great woman.' Then he closed his eyes and died.

He could have lasted another decade. And Birdie felt robbed by the neglect of the doctors. She would have nobody to talk with now. Nobody to tell her secrets to any more. No one to nurse in the king-size bed that had come all the way from Athlone. She would have nobody to make buns for. And she didn't. She never made another bun in her life.

But the thing that enraged her most of all was that she had not expected him to die in that moment, so she had not told him how Sister Bernard had upset her, or why she had upset her, or what she had said to upset her.

The Vet with his arse to the fire and his bottle of stout, and his gramophone box playing new recordings of Puccini. Birdie at the cooker concocting a feast. Soup from the gizzards of chickens. Soufflés of pineapple and cream. Gussie sitting in the dark on the bottom step of the stairs, listening to her whisking the cream and waiting for her to call him into the kitchen and lick the spoon. Waiting for his life to begin. But it never did.

Whoosh!

Why is that? Who knows? But isn't it funny that sometimes only Eugene remains. Yes. Eugene is still there. That's funny. That someone so unexpected would be the last one to leave. But for certain, she's lying there in the bed, and there's a great softness in the dawn light and a lovely sweet smell in the room, and as true as God's in heaven, she can hear the soft notes of the harmonium.

Eugene is still playing in the attic and under the stairs and beneath the floorboards of every room in the house.

That's a sign if ever there was one. Alex.

GUSSIE

I

SO THAT WAS IT. Alex in the open fields chasing bulls. Birdie in the kitchen making apple dumpling in the new pressure cooker. Gussie sitting on the stairs, listening for a heartbeat that was not his own. Whoosh.

Hard to imagine a psychiatric ward with bars on the windows, and little Gussie inside looking out like a confused rabbit in a hutch. Surely he never thought it would go that far, did he? Did he ever imagine that all those years behind closed doors, refusing to go out into the fresh air, could only lead to trouble and he'd end up walking around in a dressing gown, with everybody staring at their food or staring out the window or staring at each other? Of course it was only for a week. Doctor Gogarty said that. Or was it a month? Not long, in any event.

Gogarty was an odd fish. A dapper little man in a pinstripe suit with lizard's eyes behind silver-rimmed glasses. He had no hair at all. Not even eyebrows. The surface of his bald head was as smooth as the bonnet of a car, and he had an amber ring on his index finger. A cloud of eau de cologne trailed along the corridor after him. When he gave

Birdie his hand she shook it, and it felt like the callused paw of a wild animal. She was wondering how a doctor the size of a milk churn could have such hands. Maybe he does a lot of gardening.

'So there you go.'

That's what he kept saying. You'd think he'd have a more consoling phrase. You'd think they'd teach them something about talking to the relatives in their psychiatric school or wherever they go to become doctors.

At least Doctor Hilary had soft hands. She was in her early thirties and had short hair, like rusted leaves, and it was tossed about her white freckled face in a dishevelled manner that suggested meticulous arrangement.

Young professional women nowadays spend a lot of money trying to look like they just walked out of the shower. But she was kind. And she wore a white coat, like a normal doctor, and a stethoscope hung around her neck, and her fingers played with it as if it was a string of pearls.

Birdie met Doctor Hilary on the corridor, the first time she went to visit Gussie. The doctor was clip-clopping down the corridor, like a model on a catwalk as Birdie stared out the window. She stopped and stood there before her in her white starched rigour and her halo of rusty hair, and stared at Birdie for an eternity. Oh yes, that out-of-the-shower look. Smelling of shampoo. And sucking a pencil.

'You must be Mrs Delaney,' says she.

'That's correct, Miss. I mean Doctor.'

'Right ... OK ... Right.'

And she just smiled and walked on. Clip-clopping out through the swing doors. Still, she was better than your man. What was he called? Fogarty or something. Gussie would like the lady doctor. Not so different from Louise.

Especially around the haunches. Yes. That's what Doctor Hilary had. It was a bit of Louise around the haunches. Leggy and feminine in a clear-headed way. Things Birdie had never quite mastered.

During that week Birdie often marvelled at all that therapy they do with people in those hospitals. She wondered was there any sense to it. Poking at the past. Pulling things from under stones that would better be left where they were.

When Gussie was six, he used to catch bees in a jam jar. He loved that game. He thought the bees were beautiful. The black and yellow fur. And at seven she often saw him sitting in the old shed where the Vet kept his animal medicines, listening to the young swallows in nests under the eaves squealing for their mother to bring food. And then there was the cat. Jesus. That's the kind of story Gogarty would pick fucken holes in.

Birdie got him the cat. A tiny ball of black fluff, with two little eyes, that came in an orange box. When they let it out on the kitchen floor, it was so frightened that it tried to go out the window immediately. It jumped onto the table, and then fell back onto a red-hot ring on the cooker. It was only for a second, but the cat let out a scream of pain that sounded like a soul roasting in hell. Eventually it went behind the washing machine and refused to come out. They could smell the burning flesh and fur. Gussie got into a terrible state. He tried desperately to get the cat out, to see how badly she was hurt. But the space between the washing machine and the cupboards was too narrow for him to get his hand in and grip her. He could only see her eyes staring out from the dark. All day in school he cried his eyes out thinking about the cat. Even Birdie supposed that the hot ring had done mortal damage.

But there was no need in the wide world to be bothered. Birdie had the cat on her lap when he came home. She was drinking milk from a saucer on the table. Not a need in the world for the poor boy to be upset.

Nobody asked questions in those days. Things weren't analysed. People didn't get counselling just because they saw a few dead cats. When bad things happened you tried to get over them, forget them and move on. And a mother was a mother. Her job was simple.

Birdie just tried to make things right. She took away nightmares. She left him in bed when he had a temperature and brought comics home to him. She made him hot drinks. Hot drinking chocolate, and sometimes punch with real whiskey.

'It will put hairs on your chest,' she used to say.

She knitted jumpers. Bought him buckled sandals in the summertime, and gave him clean underwear every Saturday night, and fixed his tie, and rubbed his cheeks with a damp towel like a mother cat. She made apple dumplings and potato cakes, and stews with lashings of gravy and she always had juicy necks of lamb in the oven. She made pear tarts and flans and soufflés with real cream and she made soups from real chickens and vegetables. She made all sorts of buns in trays with different jams in the bottoms, and even buns out of Rice Krispies mixed with chocolate. She made thick pancakes coated with butter, and dusted with sugar, one on top of the other. A mountain of them on a plate in the oven. So there wasn't much in that for the psychiatric team to get their teeth into.

And above all else she prayed. She prayed for him at all times and hours, and especially when he was doing his exams. The Primary Certificate in national school. The

Intermediate Certificate, and the Leaving Certificate in the secondary college.

After that he went to university. And Birdie went to church. Who could count all the mornings Birdie knelt at the altar. A penny candle flickering at the feet of the Blessed Virgin. And though he scraped through his BA and his Higher Diploma in Education by the skin of his teeth, she rejoiced nonetheless, as if he had been awarded the Nobel Prize for Science.

Little did she ever think that she'd be praying for him at the hour of his death. Little did she know what was up the road on that Sunday morning when he came from the hospital to visit her. A male nurse waiting in the car outside. Gussie came in and tried to give her an account of what was happening to him in the hospital. She stared at the wall for twenty solid minutes and all she could do was wonder what did she do wrong. What terrible neglect on her part had caused her golden boy to end up in a mental asylum?

She made the tea. Gussie smoked one cigarette after another until she had to open the kitchen door. She could hardly breathe. She wanted to hold him, but she was too old.

2

IT WAS THE SAME when the Vet died. Alex could never drink hospital tea, which came around every afternoon in a huge silver teapot already mixed with milk, lukewarm and without any kick to it. The trolley never stopped at Alex Delaney's bed. Instead, Birdie would hand him a bun from her basket, a coconut bun, and she would pour a cup of tea from her own green thermos flask. Every day she brought him a flask of freshly brewed tea, from the finest Assam leaves available in McNamee's swanky grocery store, where they still had a bell on the door that tinkled as you entered, and still had large drawers of real tea behind the sagging counter.

But the end was unexpected. It happened in a flash. It was two in the afternoon. Alex was halfway through the bun. There was about half of it left in his hands. And it was crumbling onto the bed sheets. His eyes were closed. She knew he was sleeping. He often did that. Fell asleep for a moment or two in mid-sentence. And then he would return.

'Don't spill crumbs on the sheets,' says she.

That woke him suddenly and he said sorry, and then he looked at her. He looked into her. He looked through her. He was only a skeleton in the bed. As if a tornado had swept through him. And he was exhausted. And his skull sank into the pillow like an egg in a basket of straw. But he reached out a bony limb and patted her on the head. He smiled so intensely that she wanted to hold him, and hug him, but she felt too old.

'I'll get a tissue,' says she and she went away, just for a second towards the door. She was going to get a tissue from the communal kitchen and gather up the crumbs from the bedclothes, but she heard the slightest little noise behind her as she walked away from the bed. The noise he sometimes made when they were making love. The sleepiest of songs that his heart sometimes sang, to say he was happy, and she knew even before she turned around that there was only a scattering of bones left on the clinical bed, and that she was alone in the room and in the world.

She missed her last hug. And there she was again in the same position when Gussie came from the mental place, like he used to come to her when he fell out of a tree, or hurt his knee, or ran his bicycle under the wheels of Father Finnegan's motorcar. And the urge inside her to hold him was monstrous. To smother him with kisses like a thousand petals falling off the wild rose bushes on the avenue. It was making the knuckles of her little white claws burn with pain as she clenched the edge of the kitchen table. But Gussie just sucked his cigarette to the last poisonous breath of smoke. Deep into his lungs.

And then he left. And she saw him to the door and let him peck her on the cheek. The nurse was asleep in the car. A black shining Nissan Primera. Or was it a Volkswagen Golf?

Something anyway.

'It's great jobs they have,' Birdie says. 'They can afford such lovely cars.'

3

GUSSIE LOVED FLOWERS. He plucked them from the Vet's rose bushes. Roses as big as oranges. He took as many as he could hold and brought them to Birdie with a smile on his face. She was polishing the tiles outside the front door, with Cardinal polish.

'Mammy,' says he, shielding his eyes from the sun and stretching out his hands with the roses.

'Your father will have your guts for garters, Gussie, for stealing his roses,' she said. His hands were bleeding. Not a good sign.

Gussie got a summer job as a night porter in the hospital when he was a teenager. Fetching glasses of water in the middle of the night for old men with lung diseases. He was getting morbid. Emptying aluminium night jars from under the beds in the male ward every morning and checking the amount of fluid and writing the amount of ounces on each chart. When people died, he wheeled their bodies to the mortuary on a steel trolley. A grim voyage, through the maternity unit and out into the backyard. All in the middle of the night, so that the young mothers wouldn't know the dead were passing by where their little babies were sleeping. Though they must have been suspicious. They must have sniffed the air occasionally as they queued for their morning showers.

That's how he earned his first money. Wheeling the dead through the black wind of the mortuary yard.

Standing under the bare bulb of the mortuary fridge.

He'd be there alone with the cold skulls and the wax faces. And the small white eyelids of children and the yellow cheeks of fresh women whose livers had been eaten by cancer. Not a pretty sight. Serenity perhaps. When all the suffering and anxiety of dying was over. Maybe that's what attracted him. The serenity.

It was a hot summer. And he slept in the daytime, with the window wide open and the curtains closed. Big bluebottles buzzing like demented helicopters, and bouncing off the ceiling as if they were trying to kill themselves. A breeze shaking the curtain and the sound of tractors filling the room. But Gussie slept. And then at seven each evening, when girls on bicycles were coming from swimming at the lake, and the young lads his own age were togging out for football matches in the Chapel meadow, all sunburnt and thirsty, Gussie was putting on a brown porter's coat, with green lining on the collar and dreaming of God knows what or whom.

'Mammy,' he used to say sometimes, in the middle of the night when he was only nine or ten years old, 'I'm nervous.'

Oh indeed, we're all nervous.

When the Vet was away in Galway, or Cork, Birdie would let him into her bed sometimes and she'd lie awake as he burrowed under the blankets and glued himself to her. Oh yes, she'd whisper, we're all nervous.

4

BIRDIE NEVER FORGOT a certain warm summer night long ago, when she was a child and everything was still and moonlit, and she could hear all the insects, and she lay stretched on the bed with the windows wide open. The air was warm and the night was so utterly still and silent that even the cat creeping over the tin roof of the backyard shed would waken the dead. That was a long time ago. Birdie was only a child, when Ireland was still licking its wounds after the Civil War, and Europe was an architectural and financial ruin after the Great War. Not that Birdie knew anything about that at the time.

The children of Ireland were barely aware that the continent of Europe was any closer than Mars. They were already enveloped in the damp and musty embrace of a New Ireland. The State of Secrets. Eamon de Valera's long coat throwing its shadow everywhere. And in her bedroom there was an invisible man behind the curtain. He was always there. From the beginning. Behind the curtain. No wonder Birdie was nervous.

One night Daddy was spinning the knob of the wireless in search of English voices. Birdie was thinking of the invisible man. She knew he was there, somewhere, in the darkest corners of the house. Sometimes he had a moustache and he shouted and crackled in the wireless. Sometimes he had green slitty eyes. Like the alligator in her picture book about life in the jungle.

She didn't understand the drama on the wireless, but her daddy seemed frightened enough and the minute it was over, he flicked off the switch and ordered her to bed, and she ran up and said a decade of the rosary at her bedside in a state of terrible agitation.

She was lying on the starched sheets. The horsehair of the bed squeaking underneath her in the manner she detested, and the moon spreading a long shaft of light diagonally from the window across the room and hitting her shoes on the floor beside the wall. The night was warm.

She slept. But only for a short while. The night changed. Clouds from the Atlantic pushed across the little island of Ireland, and there came a sudden wind that ruffled the curtains and woke little Birdie from her slumber.

She screamed for half an hour, even while her daddy, in an attempt to release her from her nightmare of terror, stripped off her clothes and bathed her body in the bed with cold, wet towels. Who was it, Daddy? she wondered. He tried to reassure her. It was only 'the invisible man', he said. Don't worry. He won't be back.

So we're all nervous. Why wouldn't we be?

Forever afterwards life was a struggle of fastidious self-preservation. Round-the-clock alertness regarding any movement more suspicious than grass growing. She was keeping at bay the persistent possibility that an unwanted guest was lurking behind the curtain, or behind the remote glow of the Milky Way, who might come and steal her purse, if not her very life. So don't talk to Birdie about being nervous!

When she was a teenager, she often opened her daddy's shoelaces, as he lay exhausted on his bed when he returned from a week's work, droving cattle from the plains of Mayo down hidden by roads towards the fairs of Athenry and Ballinasloe. She would take the ball of money from his left shoe and put it in the amber-coloured sugar bowl that lay empty on the kitchen dresser. And when she was finished washing his clothes in the backyard, she would count it. Then, with a half-crown piece in the palm of her hand, she'd slip out to the public house on the corner and buy a bottle of whiskey and carry it home in a brown paper bag.

Her daddy, by now stretched on the bed, snored at the ceiling. His enormous weight bending the wire-based mattress as if it was a hammock, and the closed eyelids on his face reminding her of a beached whale in her picture book about life in the oceans.

She was always glad when Daddy came home. He was the biggest living animal she knew. And if the universe was full of invisible enemies, then the safest place to be was under the dubious protection of that enormous sleeping drunk. No matter what the cost. She ate little in those years, and her physical frame was so small that the neighbours remarked with anxiety that she was in danger of falling into an early grave. But she was simply nervous. So how many signs does a mother need?

5

BUT THERE WAS one person Birdie almost forgot about. Louise. Oh Christ. Louise. Birdie did forget about her. For years. Which was not an easy thing to do. Because Louise mattered more than anything to Gussie when he was in his twenties. With her big blue eyes and her high cheekbones and her long brown hair. But it was the smile that seduced people. That glow of pure compassion. And then, out of the blue, Louise returns.

Louise enters the room in a dress of snow. She's there dancing to the organ music. A Victorian dress, with lace at the waist and hem. Almost transparent because of the thin nature of the material. Fine net sleeves and a flared skirt. Christ, she's so wonderful. And to be twirling around in the room. Twirling to the organ of Mr Devine.

Gussie was terribly excited when he found her. He insisted Birdie get on the bus to Galway immediately. And she did. And they met in a grotty pub on the quays. Sacred Heart of Jesus, Louise was enormous! Looked down on everyone! And the pub was small and smoky. A den of stale air where middle-aged men with blotchy skin and baggy black trousers and corduroy jackets the colour of mud clutched the bar in the last stages of alcohol addiction. Wallowing in remorse.

Birdie had no patience with them. No tolerance for drunken bowsies. Red noses and white marble domes with thin lines of greasy hair combed with sad attention in the men's toilets. Sacred Heart of Jesus, what are you bringing her in here for? But it wasn't Gussie. It was Louise who knew the pub.

– Arah for godsake, Birdie, will ye quit yer ould talking there and have yerself an ould glasseen of a drink –

Then he started bringing her home, and Birdie pulled out all the stops. She spent hours in the kitchen cooking things for them. All classes of sauces to sweeten the Galway girl.

Gussie singing in the bathroom and flossing his teeth on a Saturday morning. They were going to visit the Vet in the hospital. And then Louise and Gussie would go shopping for the day. The pair of them. Like lovers. Shopping in Galway. It was hard to believe.

– Yerrah not at all, girleen, sure it's not hard to believe at all at all. –

Who said that? Birdie sits up in the bed. Cocks her head. Am I awake or dreaming?

– You're wide awake, girleen, – says Louise.

Birdie opens her eyes. Behold Louise. There she is at the foot of the bed. Oh Christ I hope I'm dreaming, because Louise is at the foot of the bed.

– Yerrah will you shtop yer complaining there girleen, sure I'm only come to lighten yer load and cheer you up. –

I'm dreaming, Birdie thinks.

– Yer not dreaming. How could you be dreaming and me here telling ye that yer wide awake? –

Birdie wants to get out of the bed; call someone on the phone. Get the police. How did you get in if I'm not dreaming?

– What time is it? – inquires the woman in white. Snow-white in lace frills. Lovely Louise, and larger than ever.

– I was behind the curtain there for years, – says she.

What were you doing there?

– I was looking for a top; an old-fashioned calico print. Isn't that funny? And do you know, Gussie was with me and we were in this girls' shop, and I was in and out of the curtained corner with jumpers and jackets and dresses that tightened in here, at the bustline, and be jeepers, Birdie, do you know what I'm going to tell you, but that son of yours, that ladeen what's now stretched out in his fine oak coffin, his hands were shaking as he fingered all the pretty lace things on the rack. Now for ye! And how long ago is that, would you say? –

Fifteen years, Birdie said. Fifteen years.

– Jeepers Birdie, 'tis only like yesterday. –

Fifteen years.

– Chríost Rí, is it that long? But sure I'm back for the funeral. Amn't I?

– Do you know what I got in the end, Birdie? I got a cream dress with a high neck and an orange mohair shawl. What do you think of that?

– And it was me started him on muesli, Birdie. Did ye not know that? Oh aye. On account of the bowels. And on fruit and yogurt. I thought it would help. Though he claimed it was bad for the health. Too much is as bad as too little he'd say. Rubbish says I, Birdie. Rubbish.

– By the way, what's the music? –

That's Mr Devine, says Birdie. He's up the chimney with his organ.

– Glorious music, Birdie. Glorious!

– I was his Madonna. You know that, Birdie? I took him from the bath gown he was folded in, like a child, and I made him new and sparkling. Smelling of almonds. –

How did you do it? Birdie heard herself ask.

– The secrets of me fingers, – says the ghost. – Bringing him across the landscape of his own body for the first time. Showing him continents he had only heard rumours of. Taking his body and making it mine. Isn't that the riddle now, Birdie? –

Are you alive or dead? Birdie heard herself say, though she said nothing. The beautiful ghost stretched herself across the bed at Birdie's feet.

– Well now, you figure that out, girleen. You figure it out for yourself. –

Tell me the colour of his eyes. If you're Louise, you must know him. You must know the colour in his eyes. Please tell me. Please.

– Oh I knew him all right to be sure to be sure. Looka now. Wan night he sat up on the mattress in me flat in the Claddagh and I daubed lipstick on his mouth and did his eyebrows with heavy black pencil. He looked like a garish puppet behind the glass in the arcade down at Salthill. And then I threw off me green silk slip and I flung it at him and says I, if you can't be a man be a woman. Do ye want to hear more, Birdie? Do ye? –

No, she heard herself say.

– Well, I ordered him to put it on. And I declare to gawd it was only the beginning. But you know as well as I do, Birdie, he's like a man with no eyes. He got it hard to find anything in the latter end. Poking around one night between me legs with his finger, and he couldn't find the hole. Can ye credit that? I says to him, will we put on the light and I'll give you a map.

– But d'ye know what I am going to tell ye, Birdie girl? I was stretched one night over an Indonesian coffee table, like I am stretched now over your ten wee toes, and he starts poking, and there's this elephant in the corner, a dancing elephant, and there's this big bowl of butter, butter if you don't mind on the floor, and between one thing and the other, between the elephant and the butter and the poking, we broke the glass and I cut me bum and he had to run downstairs to wash the wound, for you could get terrible infections from an Indonesian coffee table. –

What's an Indonesian coffee table? Birdie heard herself ask.

– Well, – says the long-legged spirit, – sure if you don't know, how would I know! –

And she laughed. Gorgeous, young, healthy laugh. Body shaking on Birdie's bed. Touchable milk-white breasts inside the lace bodice. And she turned her head sideways on the bedspread to look up at Birdie. Laughing. Laughing like a wee girl.

– Ah Mammy, – says she, lancing poor Birdie with such a beguiling smile that Birdie had to scream. And she tried to scream. Struggled to scream. And then she did. She screamed.

No she didn't. She heard herself scream. And then she was awake. And the room was empty.

Oh Jesus Christ, if only the Vet was with her now. He'd mind her. He'd look after her. Lying awake all night. Waiting to bury her only son. And then falling asleep and finding invisible men lurking behind the fucken curtain, and a fucken whore lying on the bed laughing at her. She didn't need to be told anything about what Gussie did or didn't do with Louise. She had her own life. Jesus Christ, she had the Vet. He wasn't always bewildered in a hospital bed with cot sides to protect him from falling out and a tube stuck up his mickey to let the piss out of his bladder without him knowing it. He wasn't always like that. He was the Vet.

Didn't she dance tangos and foxtrots and quicksteps around the golf club while Mrs Hannigan was being carried to the car by Vincent Goldsmith, for rumpy-pumpy or whatever they call it nowadays, in the back of his Zephyr?

For Christ's sake, the Vet was a man of the world. As he

used to say himself, just because the photographs are in black and white, doesn't mean we didn't live in Technicolour.

Alex would cross galaxies in search of someone like Birdie. That's what he used to say to her. No matter what black hole, or nebula of inarticulate emotion she was lost in, he would come like Yuri Gagarin in his Sputnik, and he'd find her. What about the time he brought her to London? The cocktail bar? Well?

The suits and the long dresses. The chubby manager in his green double-breasted tweeds fussing over Mr Delaney. Alex had a coherence about him that people loved to lean on. An air of authority. And no end of money. Good aftershave.

The world is divided into men who love women, and men who can't. That's what he said.

Oh, Birdie, the virgins of the forest said, he's divine! Charming, polished and stylish. He's so commanding. He has his two feet on the ground. He has. And he never lost his sense of humour. But most of all you could tell him anything and it didn't unsettle him.

They checked into the hotel in London in the early hours of the morning. They had taken the night train from Holyhead. Alex signed the book with his Parker fountain pen, while Birdie perched on a sofa in the foyer and gripped her handbag as if she was clutching a lifebelt on the deck of the *Titanic*. She was terrified. London if you don't mind. And they weren't a year married. Now that was a weekend in Technicolour!

Ten minutes later Birdie was stretched on the bed upstairs in a swanky hotel bathrobe, and Alex was sitting upright and expectant in a green plastic chair beside the window. The tall buildings of London town behind him. A cactus on the coffee table beside him, like a little green hedgehog. There was a wireless above the bed with ivory knobs. She fumbled with it until she found orchestral music. The strings of gentlemen in dinner jackets. Everything was velvet. It was hardly nine o'clock, but she ran the hot water in the bath and he actually took off his clothes in front of her, and when he wasn't looking she dribbled some of her perfume into the cloud of steam and then, without thinking, she poured the entire bottle in. Alex, all white and bony, climbed into the tub and suddenly he sniffed the air and it nearly knocked him out.

'Sweet Divine Jesus,' he roared.

He hopped round the hotel room pretending he was scalded by the water or poisoned by the perfume, and Birdie said she never laughed as much in years.

'I couldn't get into that,' says he 'I'd smell like French knickers for the rest of the day.'

Get in, says she. And in he got. So don't tell Birdie about bowls of butter!

After the bath he towelled himself and said he was going to leave. He put on his soft felt hat and threatened to walk out the door, naked but for the hat, and Birdie thought it was priceless. He still had the hat on when he sat on the side of the bed and slipped his hand underneath her dressing gown, folded himself into her, like a snake, and slithered all over the bed, as the velvet voice in the distance above them warned of snow in the Hebrides and anticyclones coming in from the Atlantic. So don't talk to Birdie about Indonesian coffee tables or dancing elephants.

– Alright then, girleen, I swear I won't mention them again, – says snow-white Louise from behind the curtain, and then she comes out and the room seems to be turning white. The walls and the bedspread and the wardrobe and the television set. Everything is turning white. And Louise is coming towards her. The only two things that are not white are the big blue eyes in the Snow Queen coming closer and closer, so that Birdie thinks she's going to kiss her. And she does.

I should wake up now, Birdie thinks. That kiss should wake me. But it doesn't. And suddenly Victorian Louise seems sad, and she sits on the bottom of the bed with her back to Birdie and she says – I know what you're going to ask me. –

What?

– You want to know why I went away! –

Yes.

– He was too careful, Birdie. He was like a tailor, threading a needle. –

What do you mean?

– What do I mean? Sure, Birdie girl, how would I know what I mean if you don't know who I am? –

Birdie was looking at the broad back of the woman at the bottom of the bed. You're Louise, she heard herself say.

The Snow Queen turned around. First the shoulders, then the face, with white curls falling either side of the cheeks and eyes like pools of ocean blue ...

– Who? –

Christ Jesus, Birdie heard herself scream. But she didn't scream. And she didn't wake. And the big girl at the end of the bed came closer. So close Birdie wanted to kiss her again. Kiss her and fondle her and hold her close for a little while longer. She tried to reach out but her body wouldn't move. That's when she woke up. The curtain moving in a tiny breeze. The bedroom door ajar.

BIRDIE

I

WHAT TIME IS IT? She doesn't know. She listens. Not a sound. And the room is so white. She takes a peek through the curtains. It's just as she thought. A blanket of snow covers the earth. A blue sky over it all with a rich sliver of moon over the beech trees in the distance. And the quietness of snow is always unexpected and severe.

What day is it? She can't remember. She tries to find religious services on the transistor radio beside her pillow. No good. Then she tries the small television at the end of the bed. No. Not even a picture. Must be broken.

She potters around the top of the landing, looking for vests. Then she walks along the corridor to the toilet. It's wonderful to pass water. To have no leakage overnight. To have no dizziness or lightness in the head.

Fine. She is dressed and fully awake in her room, and she sits at the window and looks out again at the blanket of snow. Still some darkness in the far trees. A white stillness on the world. No neighbour stirring. There are no neighbours out here. No lights in the distance. But what time is it? Or what day is it?

The only neighbours were the Kellys, who farmed the land and lived in an old cottage on the opposite side of the road. But they are long gone. The cottage down near the main road is falling apart. The garden overgrown with nettles. The windows broken. The gutters thick with weeds, and ivy creeping up the walls and around the windows. For some reason Birdie thinks it's Sunday.

Long ago the church would be packed to the gills on a Sunday morning, and the entire population of the parish would be out on the roads. Birdie used to sit on the bed and give a running commentary to the Vet as he sucked oranges and lay in the sheets beside her. She'd tell him what car was passing on the main road. Was it going slow? Who was in it? God bless your eyesight, he'd say.

Birdie thought the new hip would make all the difference. That it would take away her nervousness. But to tell the truth, when she returned to Ballinasloe the first thing she discovered was that the television had shrunk. Well, that didn't do her nerves any good. And then she noticed that someone had changed all the photographs on the walls. And there were sheets missing from the hot press. And the papers belonging to the house, the insurance documents, and the forms for her social welfare money were all upside down. Someone had been visiting. The invisible man was at it again. His threatening presence behind the curtain.

Birdie rushes to the statue of the Virgin, and lights a candle on the saucer, and with the intensity of a child, she sits on the edge of the bed, squeezes her hands together, and begs the Virgin not to leave her alone. To send her the angels, or the Vet, or even Mr Devine on his organ. She cries. She works her breath into a climax. And then it's gone. It's over.

Nothing to worry about. Just a turn. Like blood pressure. An inward convulsion as the tinker woman said. And now she wipes away her tears and goes out onto the landing to negotiate the stairs.

Down the same stairs she goes, very nifty, one at a time, easy and gentle. Smiling defiantly on each step. Each move is a victory. She feels triumphant, because this morning she is not crawling down on her bum. No, sir. She is home. And nobody or nothing will ever take her away from her home again.

She reaches the hall. The level ground. And she stands erect in her own house.

'So,' says she. 'It's time to make the dinner.'

Not that she thinks it's the middle of the day or anything like that. Birdie is no fool. She knows what day it is. She knows how early it is. But she wants to make dinner.

That's not a crime, is it? She finds a potato and a bowl of cabbage in the fridge. It's been there since the week before. All she has to do is heat it in the microwave. And from the freezer box she takes a meat burger. Then she stands over the pan watching it sizzle.

The burger is ready in a few minutes. She puts it on the plate but she can't understand why it's rock-hard. Then she goes to the microwave, only to find that the cabbage and potato are still cold. Maybe something is wrong with the machine.

Onwards to the drawing room, plate in hand, where she sits on the sofa, turns on the television, expecting to see the omnibus edition of *Eastenders*. She always watches the reruns of her favourite soaps on a Sunday. They're more enjoyable the second time round, and easier to follow.

Dinner doesn't satisfy her. It's just not nice. Too cold. Too hard. And she can't find anything on the television except news programmes. So she waits for the football matches to begin. That's how she has spent her Sunday afternoons for two decades. Watching the matches. Doesn't matter what it is. Soccer. Rugby. Gaelic. She likes those athletes in their prime rising in the air for the balls. But there is no match! It just so happened that on this particular Sunday not one of the eight television stations is showing a football match. Now isn't that a curious thing?

She watches on, for another half an hour, hoping to see film stars in bikinis, or quizmasters, or the posh lady up to her arse in farmyard muck talking about the value of organic material around a rose bush. But nothing doing! All she can find is the friggin' news. Breakfast news. Yes. Breakfast news. Because it's fucken breakfast time.

OK. That doesn't matter, because in fact, what she really wants is the Oxo box. That's what she wants. And it's on the kitchen table. She saw it there when she was heating the cabbage.

You see that's why she was getting the heebie-jeebies about the house being empty. That's why she couldn't sleep all night. The Oxo box lying out where anyone could have gawked into it. She had gone to bed and left the Oxo box on the table. That's why she was disturbed in her dreams.

She turns off the television and sees her reflection on the screen. An old woman in her dressing gown. Sleepless and frightened at the dawn of a winter's day, with a frozen burger and stale cabbage lying on the plate in her lap. Still haunted by an invisible man.

There was no more she could do for Gussie. That's not what troubled her. She had always done her best for Gussie. But it was the Vet she had failed. Because she didn't tell him everything. In a sense, she didn't tell him anything.

Birdie staggers down the hall towards the kitchen, her hands outstretched towards the Oxo box.

Momo! she cries. Momo!

2

THE OXO BOX contains the oldest photographs in the history of Birdie Waters. A few dozen frayed images in sepia-brown, black and white, or stubborn negatives, in which an Edwardian gentleman with whiskers stands to attention beside a little girl in a white dress who sits on a chair beside him. There is an image of the little girl in Dublin, outside a shop that sells tobacco, and Birdie can see white pigeons at the girl's feet. Dozens of them in a line along the back of the bench. Lots and lots of images captured on O'Connell Bridge, and many formal poses by uncles and aunts who are long dead. Whiskers. Wan-faced women. Children in states of attention and fear as they gazed at the camera. And hidden beneath them all, at the bottom of the box, is the only single image that still exists on earth of little Momo. The only record that she ever lived.

Just nine months after the invisible man spoke on the wireless and then hid all night behind the bedroom curtain, Bernadette Waters gave birth. She called the little girl Momo, but the fun didn't last long. The doctors were worried. Little Momo was weak and didn't breathe well, and she was taken away to be scrutinized and watched over by nuns.

Birdie only saw her through the glass windows on the corridor of the nursery. And the nuns said that Birdie had neglected herself during the confinement, which didn't help the baby. So in a way it was Birdie's fault that Momo was sick.

Such an isolated little creature, Birdie thought, when she looked at Momo's ivory fingers the size of matchsticks, and her eyes still closed to the world. Her magical little button of a nose.

Three months Birdie spent in that convent, scrubbing floors, though she was only thirteen. That's when Birdie went off buttermilk for life. Never again, she vowed. The buttermilk every day was the worst part of the pregnancy. And no one came to visit her. Not even Daddy. And the only ones who were interested in her were the nuns and the police, and that was for different reasons. They dismantled her. Poking and probing to see would she tell them anything.

Sister Bernard was a young nun then. She kept saying that it would take time, but that Birdie would come round to the idea of an adoption eventually. She was only a child herself.

'Who ever done this,' says Sister Bernard, 'has destroyed you. Can you understand that?'

But Birdie thought it was wonderful. She was a woman. She was a mother. She would soon become the dairy queen.

'Will I have milk soon?' Birdie wondered.

'Of course you won't,' Sister Bernard said. 'You're only thirteen.'

Momo helped Birdie forget everything. Forget where Momo came from, or who shook the curtain, and who stole the cookie, and how it all happened. Soon, she hoped, the cosmos within her would begin to pour out life to her hungry little monster, her gorgeous little Momo.

'You can't call her Momo,' Sister Bernard said. 'It's not a name.'

And as Birdie waited each day for the wonderful flood tide of cosmic love to start flowing through her breasts, the world actually became very narrow. They squeezed her into a tiny room without the infant, and they only let her go to the nursery once a day. Her breasts hurt as if someone had beaten them with a rod. But no milk came.

Life in the convent was organized by numbers. Times. Clocks. Places to go. Things to scrub. A life without climaxes. And cheap curtains.

She complained to Sister Bernard that maybe Momo was missing her and that she should be there more often with her. But Sister Bernard only sneered. At night the baby's face went beetroot-red from screaming in the nursery. Birdie dangled a yo-yo beside the glass, when Momo was watching, but it only made things worse. She wanted to get a doll but the nun said it was far too soon for dolls, and there was no point pampering the baby since her new mammy was coming in a matter of a few weeks and she would take care of all that.

Some of the younger nuns did give Birdie a chance to hold little Momo, when Sister Bernard was sleeping. Birdie's feet slapped the linoleum all through the night as she paced up and down, singing about elephants and piggies and the three little bears. And the young nuns pitied her.

'Are you not exhausted, ye poor creature?' they'd say. But Birdie wasn't exhausted. Not if she was to stay up all night. It was better than shaking that yo-yo at the other side of the glass window and frightening the little creature in her cot.

Sometimes there were parties on the street outside and

Birdie could see people from the nursery window, as they strolled home in the dark. Men like wolves stalking the streets and women with their arms linked, giggling and following behind.

She could hear the bottles and glasses clinking in the pub across the street on Saturday nights. She could hear the front doorbell downstairs whenever someone came to the door of the convent, and she prayed each time that it would be Daddy, and not someone saying they wanted to be little Momo's new mammy.

'Momo,' says she, in the refectory one morning. There was no one to ask and no one to tell. So she said Momo, one morning and that was it.

'I'm calling you little Momo.'

She informed the nun the next time she was up to the nursery.

'Oh don't be ridiculous,' the nun said, 'sure she has already been christened Jennifer!' and then she burst out laughing. But Momo was cross. Really cross. And getting worse. Hours without end she could scream into all the nuns' faces, till the holy women went from guilt to rage and wanted to dash little Momo's brains against the radiator on the wall. And then five minutes afterwards the child would fall asleep, and Birdie would be astonished at how much she loved her, and wanted her, and needed her. Like little Momo was the best thing ever happened. She'd sit there beside where Momo was sleeping until the nuns shooed her off and told her not to be wasting so much time in dilly dreams with the baby. The child was seven weeks old.

'Her new mammy is coming on Sunday,' the nun said.

You said that last week, Birdie thought. You lying fucken bitch!

'Just go away, Bernadette Waters. Go and get to your bed.'

Birdie went to her cubicle in the dormitory and read herself bedtime stories. *The Wind in the Willows*. 'The Princess and the Pea'.

And she couldn't wait till little Momo had teeth.

Yes. Teeth. Because there was no way the nuns were going to take little Momo away from her then. When Momo got the teeth. No way! She'd go home to Daddy in a few weeks and everything would work out well.

Couldn't wait till Momo could talk. Till she could eat with a spoon and they'd make up baby talk together having their breakfast. The last day was a Sunday. She spent all her money on a white frilly bonnet so that Momo would look pretty for her new mammy. It was the end of March. She asked the nun could she wear her own clothes instead of the convent uniform. She was afraid that she might not look well dressed. Small things can humiliate. The nun just tut-tutted her and remarked how vain some young girls can be!

She wanted to undo the world after it happened.

To wind back the cosmos. She wanted to make it all squeeze into the zero moment of origination. The dot before time began, when there were no moving curtains or invisible men or asteroids or Milky Ways. When everything was a dot.

Little Momo's feet had gone purple. Her fingers and nails had gone purple. Her face was as empty as a full moon. Momo was gone away. And only a dead carcass remained in the cot.

There was nobody in the nursery only Birdie. There was no one to see her. And no one to say it to. No one in the kitchen or in the refectory or in the dormitory, because all the nuns and the other girls were at Sunday Mass in the Chapel. There was no one to stop her from standing there, listening, as if the dead could speak a little baby speak. No one who might pull her away from the mirror. The baby was eight weeks old. Birdie was thirteen. She went to the graveyard and got sick all over her coat, after lying on the soil and pushing her face into the mud.

'Oh,' said the nun in the infirmary, 'it's little Miss Waters! Now what has she done to her face?'

HUGHIE

I

THANK GOD FOR HUGHIE! That's all Birdie can say sometimes, and she's said it often enough. That's what she said as she stood in the middle of the hospital reception area, and it as busy as a bus station, and Birdie with not a notion what she was supposed to do or where to go. Patients escorting their loved ones to the main door. Kissing them goodbye. Visitors who had never been there before, wandering around and staring at arrows on the walls, in a daze, and looking more disturbed than the patients. Children playing with the doors of the lift. Old ladies clustering around the reception desk with useless questions about where to get buns and buses. When Hughie stepped in through the revolving doors with a small brown paper bag under his arm, no one could doubt that he was a great man, and Birdie was totally at ease with him there beside her. He walked with great confidence. He knew the building inside out.

He had been there as a patient. In and out like a yo-yo over the years. Not that Birdie would tell anyone that. Birdie could keep a secret. A confidence.

So Birdie went up and stared at the lady behind the desk.

'I want to speak to my son,' says she.

'Who?'

'My son,' says she.

'What's his name?' says Miss Busybody.

Birdie wasn't going to tell her. What business of hers was that?

But Hughie chirped in.

'Delaney,' says he. 'Gussie Delaney.'

'Second floor,' says Miss Busybody. 'Room 212. NEXT!'

Thank God for Hughie Donoghue.

In the middle of the shining floor, a man in a blue nylon work coat sat on top of a polishing vehicle. And Hughie looked smart. He wore black-laced shoes, which were well polished. He was like a retired policeman. His brown suit was wrinkled and the seat of his pants was as shiny as his shoes. But he stood out nonetheless. He had broad shoulders and the suit hung on his skeletal frame with the graceful lines of a garment well-cut from fine linen. It was his professional suit. The one he had bought in Louis Copeland's shop on his way to make the only appearance of his life on television thirty-two years earlier. Every dog has its day, as they say.

And he really did know his way around the new unit. That was the polite name for the clearing house where the daily intake of nervous wrecks was sorted out and dispatched to appropriate destinations. Alcoholics. Manic depressives. Schizophrenics. The bewildered. Or those simply suffering from emotional exhaustion. They were all categorized and sent on to the relevant units, wards, centres, medical departments or simply discharged.

So there was no need for any further questions at reception. Hughie knew exactly where Room 212 was situated.

The last door at the end of the corridor on the second floor. Great!

But Birdie couldn't manage the stairs. She stood to the rear of the lift as a tearful woman in a black plastic anorak was coaxed in by three overweight teenage girls who kept assuring her that their daddy would be disappointed if she turned back now.

Hughie's long face was blank. His brown hair was combed backwards and glued to his skull with Brylcreem. He was used to the intimacies that spill out on hospital corridors. His face had the serenity of a man who has heard everything in life twice.

They stepped out on the second floor. The lady who was being dragged to her husband tried to get out with them. But no such luck. The daughters grabbed her and pulled her back.

Birdie hopped along behind the big man. Him pacing slowly. Her behind scooting along at full speed to keep up with his long strides. It was the black leather shoes she kept looking at for comfort. She could almost see her face in them they were that shiny. And they never faltered.

Step by step in an easeful rhythm. Squeaking along the polished linoleum. And gentle. A gentle, firm step. Like a lion creeping up on the deer. As if the sound of heavy foot-falls might unease the patient before they had met.

'Poor Gussie,' she kept muttering, as they approached the room. Getting herself all excited. Imagining him lying on the bed. His back as stiff as a wooden plank. His eyes staring at the ceiling. Maybe they'd have him all drugged up and he wouldn't be able to talk to them.

And at the last moment she faltered; she couldn't do it. She couldn't go in. It was all too much. She wheeled to the window and stared out and clutched her handbag and told Hughie to go in on his own.

'What if he's naked or something?' says she.

'Ah now,' says Hughie 'after you coming all this way!'

'Tell him his mammy is out here,' says she. 'Maybe he'd come out and see me.'

Hughie didn't knock. He eased the door open as gently as a thief in the night. A warrior sneaking up on the enemy. He stood at the foot of the bed and presented a bottle of whiskey in a crumpled brown paper bag. She saw that. And then he closed the door gently.

For a long time he didn't come out. And Birdie would put her ear to the door sometimes, to see if she could hear anything. But there wasn't a sound.

Surely Gussie would be glad to see him. The big gaunt giant towering over him. His huge hands around the parcel and a single strand of brown hair falling down over his left eye. After a while she could hear the muffled voice of her son. And she was right. He sounded as if he had been dosed with drugs. Thank God she didn't go in.

2

NOT THAT THERE WAS ever anything inappropriate about her friendship with Hughie Donoghue. Make no mistake about that. And certainly not that there was the slightest – oh Jesus be her witness – not the slightest suggestion ever of anything flirtatious between the pair of them. Or cheating behind the Vet's back. Not for one second! Didn't she keep her eyes down, if he ever started that codology with her. Or she'd look away. In the warm Kerry nights. In the smoke-filled pubs. And besides, when did she ever see him again, after that week? Hardly ever. And then him and the Vet parted ways. So that was the end of it.

If there was anything, it was the music. That's what she loved about him. He had the music. The three of them had it. The Vet most of all was the dancer. And in those days it was all big bands and saxophones and smoky, crooning voices. A world of taffeta frocks and men like stallions in harness. A ballroom world. A golf-club fantasy.

But Hughie was on a different planet. His jigs and reels were like a universe unto themselves. And even though he'd sit in the corner of the bar, stiff as a poker, with his head twisted sideways to the flute, there was something uncivilized, unharnessed in the energy that his music released. Knowing Hughie was like standing beside a fire. That's what she loved about him.

Hughie was born beside the lake. Just where it turns into river and runs in torrents over the rocks towards the sea. Rivulets of brown water and white foam in every gully of the mountain. Water and music oozing from the earth in equal measure as Hughie used to say. A diviner's world.

He told her once that he could remember how the old men used to leave their flutes in the grass of the meadow on summer nights. All night the rosewood and black-wood instruments would lie silent in the damp land, until dawn, while they slowly absorbed both the sun's rays and the early morning dew rising from the grass. It tempered the wood so beautifully that when the musician came out from his breakfast and lifted the flute to his lips, there emerged a sound so mellow and light that people would say it must have been the fairies put the music in it. Or that some timbre of the earth's sleeping inhabited the rosewood overnight, imbuing it with the music of the world's dreaming.

In Cornagee, where Hughie Donoghue lived, people told a story about where music came from. There were five brothers, they said. And one of them went to the fair one day, but didn't return. Seven days passed, and seven nights, and the other brothers watched from the end of the lane and wondered where might the young fellow have gone.

Eventually on the seventh evening, there was a knock on the door. And in he came. But without bidding them a good evening or goodnight, he went straight to the loft and rummaged around till he found an old flute that had once come from an uncle in America. And he brought it down to the kitchen, shook the dust off it and began to play.

He played the most beautiful music that was ever heard. And all his brothers gazed at him in wonderment.

'Where did you learn music like that?' they asked.

But he looked at them in equal astonishment.

'I haven't a fucken clue,' says he. For he couldn't even remember where he had been for the seven nights.

There was one night in Kerry, when the Vet was asked to go out and admire some exotic breed of horse in the hills above Killorglin.

'I'll mind her till you get back,' Hughie said. 'I won't let any of these Kerry haverels be troubling her.'

It was all good fun. Harmless banter. A bit of craic.

But it was early evening, and the pub was quiet. Almost empty. They sat in the corner and he started looking into her eyes and telling her the secrets of the flute.

Flute music is like a long ribbon in the wind, says he. That's the only way he could describe it. He stood erect and blew through the long black cylinder and she could almost see the blue ribbon issue from the other end and dance around him. A ribbon getting longer and longer as he played. She could see anything he imagined. She could believe anything he said.

'It's a passion, Birdie,' says he. 'And passions like that can't be harnessed.'

Sometimes, says he, he could play so long that the ribbon grew and grew, in circles round him so that it was like a whirlpool, and he was inside it, and smothered by its soft, silky feeling.

'Such poetic talk, Mr Donoghue,' says she. 'But I know what you mean,' she said. He could feel the texture of a tune like silk in his fingers, says he.

'And the colour changes all the time,' he said. 'Slow airs are blue ribbons. Jigs and reels are like red silk. Leaping like flames. And do you know something, Mrs Delaney? Polkas for some strange reason, and I'm good at the polkas, I always see them as black.'

Then he played her a tune. A polka. 'The Dark-Haired Girl', he said was the name of it. A black polka, he said. And for a moment, when he played the flute, Birdie thought there was no other sound in the world. There wasn't even a world. It was like travelling in space. Being out there in the black ocean of eternity. Floating along in deep silence. That's how it was for a few minutes.

The evening sun slanting in the window. Glowing red. Promising another good day. He finished the tune.

'When music enters the world,' says he, 'the world withers away. And nothing exists but emptiness and ribbons of silk.'

He could be such a charming man betimes.

'That's beautiful,' she whispered. 'That's beautiful.'

The Vet was her prize, and he was out the road looking at other prize bulls or horses or goats. She couldn't remember. And she had got all she longed for. The house was coming. The new cooker. The nights in the golf club. The unspeakable and delicious delirium of respectability. But Hughie was different. It was as if he didn't care about those things. He played reels like tornadoes that week, in the smoky pubs of Listowel and Killorglin. He was a big, chiselled man with the long, angular face of Mayo folk in his grey suit. And he was always a gentleman. He never took advantage. He would take out the three pieces of black shining ebony, which he carefully assembled, screwing each one clockwise into the next. He lifted it to his lips. Spat into it once or twice. Spat on the floor. Took a long draught of his Guinness, and again, with the determination of a carpenter twisting a screw precisely into the right spot, he pressed the flute to his lips.

Jesus! Sometimes that's all Birdie could remember. The floor melted into a whirlwind, and she saw the ribbons before her two eyes. Silk ribbons. Light blue and green ribbons dancing in the air and encircling both of them.

It was like being at the beginning of a new galaxy. As he swallowed the little tumblers of whiskey that glowed like liquid amber in the light of the bar.

In between tunes he was always raising disputes and arguments about history. He had his own theories about everything.

'The question is, where did the music come from?' he declared, like an orator in parliament. 'Now some credit the fairies and some the Connaught Rangers,' says he.

Who?

'The Rangers,' says he. 'The British army's most ferocious

and finest regiment in the history of warfare. The true embodiment of Galway, Roscommon and Mayo courage for the last two centuries.'

'From the Peninsular War,' he sang, 'to the fields of Salonica, from the deserts of the Punjab to the ...'

The song trailed off. The landlady was watching him and he was uncertain of her position on ballads in celebration of the British army.

It wasn't the song concerned her, but she was fascinated nonetheless. And knowing that the Vet was out the road, and Mrs Delaney was newly married, she didn't mind coming out from behind the bar, since it was quiet yet, and she sat between the pair of them, between Hughie and Birdie, and showed no end of interest in the history of the music.

Hughie asked her to consider how many men besides his father had returned to their villages and townlands in Connaught over those centuries with a few shillings in their purse and an army flute or a fife in their kitbag?

How many had gathered in groups over the years, in dozens of different parishes, organizing themselves into marching bands, and parading on St Patrick's Day at the local church or in a summer field before a football match?

Did they remember the far world, or the terrible pity of war, when they played their marching tunes, he wondered?

Of course they did! His father and others were warriors who had seen Armageddon and the valley of death a thousand times, and they had marched into it over and over again, playing polkas and carrying their mascots high and proud. Their flags and banners. That's how they could infuse such wild fury into the music of County Roscommon.

'Nothing like that in Kerry,' he asserted.

Well, the barwoman didn't know Hughie's father, and

she didn't seem so animated by the idea that the British army had contributed so much to the development of Irish music, or that Kerry slides might be inferior to the bellicose flutes of Roscommon, but she did know that Hughie had suddenly lathered himself into a cantankerous sweat, so she took the empty Babycham glass and the empty pint glass from the small table and returned to her work.

'Same again,' says Hughie, defiantly to her back.

'And yourself, Mrs Delaney?' says the barwoman. 'Will you be having another Babycham while you're waiting for your husband?'

Birdie said she would. And Hughie leaned over and whispered something terribly crude about the lady behind the bar, but Birdie had to admit that there were times Hughie's crudities made her laugh. Then he got up suddenly and went out the back with the stride of a general. He left the door open after him, and Birdie could hear the powerful flow of his piss sinking with a ferocious splash in the open toilet in the yard outside.

'You're as healthy as a trout,' says she, when he returned.

On the last day of the honeymoon there was a change in the weather and an altered mood in the car as they motored up the countryside in slanting rain and wind blowing dead branches across their path. The Vet was quiet. He said he was tired. And Hughie, smoking in the rear of the station wagon, kept talking in riddles. As if he was hurt.

'They say me father lit a cigarette one night in a pub in Camden Town,' says he, 'and then vanished forever into a puff of smoke. Wasn't he the lucky man!'

Silence for five miles.

'Beware of the man who can't sing. He's like the blacksmith's bellows. He breathes but he's not alive.'

Another ten miles of silence. Then he told the story of the tinker woman. He started it in Gort, and kept it going all the way to Athenry.

'Did ye hear tell of the tinker woman who fell in love with the man from Skehana?' he inquired. 'Oh, very respectable man he was. Came from people that would have no truck with her kind. But anyway, he went off with her. Shacked up with her in the caravan, he did. And they got on well. Slept in the day. Loved good porter. Butter on their porridge. And the silver caravan was a cradle in the night.

'She had the silver earrings. And the horseshoe rings on her fingers that her father made out of sixpenny pieces. Chrome buckets and basins. Silver spoons. Gold bracelets. Brass and copper. Wellingtons and shawls.

'But of course she was never good enough for respectable people, was she? No. Far from it.

'The guards in a squad car at the door of the trailer one day, wanting to know did they have a licence for the television and did anyone have a tax for the van, and did anyone have a licence for the five dogs that were barking at their heels. And the lad says to the guards, "Here," he says, "I suppose we need a fucken licence for riding in the wagon as well." It was a joke. But, says the guard, "Don't you get smart with me, ye boy ye! Don't ever wan of yous get smart alecky with me."

'Well of course the lad in the caravan wanted to say, hold on a minute, guard, what do you mean, one of "yous"? Sure I'm not a tinker.' But then he thought of her behind him, hiding under the bed in her tinker's knickers, so he kept his gob shut.

'You lie down with a tinker, you pays the price. Am I right? Oh I'm fucken right alright! Anyway. It didn't end so good. 'Cos there was this night came, when they'd been drinking a fair bit, and he was out at the fire on the ditch with her father. They were just standing there, staring into the glowing embers, when there was this brightness in the sky behind them. Not a flash. Just a rich light behind their heads. And it seemed lovely for a moment. The warmth of the fire spreading into the darkness.

'And then they turned. And there was flames all over the caravan. Flames dripping down the walls like honey. Slowly dripping from the roof to the floor. Slow flames. Like blobs of honey. They couldn't see the trailer any more. There was just this big square of flame. Like a giant firelighter. And then he seen the girl. And she was coming out of the fire. And running towards him. And she was on fire. She was the fire. Running towards him, and then falling over and tumbling into the ditch where he had been soaking wattles the previous night. The wee ditch he had been soaking the wattles in. There was a drain of water there. And she was running to it. For to squelch the fire. And you could hear the water putting it out. Putting the girl out. Putting the love of his life out. Quenching her. Can you imagine the silence after that, eh?

'There'd be no cure for that now, Birdie, would there? No. All the music in China wouldn't cure that silence.'

GUSSIE

I

WHERE ELSE WOULD Gussie go? He had the loan of a car. And there he was just released from the hospital. And he didn't want to come home to Birdie. And he certainly wasn't going back to Cornagore. And he couldn't go back to Mullingar. So where else would the poor creature go, only to Hughie?

And Birdie didn't expect that Hughie was all that thrilled to see him. But it was two o' clock in the afternoon, and poor Hughie couldn't resist the idea of the public houses, and then a comfortable lift home. The pair of them were in Bernie's Tavern in Crosshill, apparently all that afternoon with their backs to the wall, and not a word out of either of them.

Like monks in Glenstal. And sometimes Hughie moving his lips in some secret conversation with himself. What was that about? His back straight as a rush, and him in his late seventies. Just staring straight ahead. And the boy beside him. Well. Maybe he was thinking of the old days. And the girl in the bar said he supped his pint as if it was buttermilk.

They probably drove home in silence too. Not of course

that Hughie would even remember that time in Kerry. Sure, to him that was only a few days' fun. Followed by another few days with more fun.

The enclosed world Birdie was entering would have meant nothing to Hughie. He didn't seem to understand marriage. He had fun all the time. Years of high jinks and capers and play-acting! An eternity of it probably! And his face bronze from the sun. That was a thing she always noticed in Kerry. The blistered, blotchy way she took the sun until her face looked like a big fat rasher. And yet Hughie was as brown as the lady blackbird. But he wouldn't remember that. Not at all. He had more to be doing over the years. And besides, it was nothing. Nothing at all. It was absolutely nothing.

So it was just the way things worked out that he happened to drive her into the hospital, and then he met Gussie and then the rest, as they say, is history.

It was quare history for Hughie, having to recite it all to the guards. Poor Hughie. They made him go over everything. Every last detail. Fucken Sherlock Holmes. Is that who they thought they were?

But it was grand to think of Hughie showing such kindness to Gussie. And bringing him home. And lighting the fire in the Stanley range. And then he untied the dog and brought him into the kitchen. Such a picture. The pair of boys. Two men and a dog. Troopers.

Gussie opened the door and stood leaning against the lattice and he stared out at the dry October evening, listening to the rustle of the chestnut leaf. Hughie told her that. He looked up into the chestnut tree, he did. And says he to Gussie, 'That will all fall be morning. All that canopy of leaf. If there's frost.'

There were circles around the pale moon floating up in the dusk.

'All that leaf will fall.' That's what Hughie said. Told Birdie every word of it in her own drawing room when it was all over.

And Gussie made himself useful with the sweeping brush. By jingo! she was proud to hear that. And tidying up some of the empty bottles that were accumulating under the dresser and under the sink, and under the sofa and in the presses and cupboards.

'I still have the wee cottage,' he explained to Birdie. 'Just the three rooms. You walk in and there's the kitchen. I have an old car seat for an armchair and sure I don't take much care of it. And off to the right is me bedroom. And up to the left, behind the chimney there's the room me mother died in. I don't go in there much now. It's all junk, Birdie. Junk. You know yourself. A lifetime of junk.'

But apparently the pair of boys had a fry. Two pans of it. Eggs. Bacon. Liver and kidneys. Mushrooms. Rashers. Even onions.

'A feast, Birdie. A feast. Who would have thought?'

All washed down with tea and followed by a plate of bread and jam. And then Hughie said he was going for a walk on the hills. And Gussie said he'd like to go with him.

So they both headed out. Put on old black coats and peaked caps and wellingtons and pushed up the hill behind the house like crows waddling towards a bucket of corn.

The mountain rising ahead of them and the clear sky promising a long, dry, frosty night.

'But he never spoke a word to me,' Hughie said.

The dog was running round in circles, listening for foxes, and watching and following badger trails. Then they came to a well. And to a holly bush. To an old shed with horse tackle that Hughie had never seen before in all the years he had travelled that path. They came to the top of the ridge where they could see into Mayo. In the long grass they saw the shadow of a badger but they stood their ground.

The badger was still. Listening. He was only three metres away from them. Hungry and frightened. It was a time of year when the females get pregnant. There's lots for the males to do. Keep her dry and warm and change the bedding. Hughie moved. The badger moved.

'Dangerous fuckers betimes,' Hughie explained. 'If they take a grip of your leg, they'd never let go. You'd have to break a stick. Only way to get them to release their jaws. The snap of the stick. They think it's the bone breaking. Won't let go till then. Fuckers.

'And I swear to Christ,' Hughie said, 'the poor boy never said a word. Not a thing. We just walked and walked.'

They walked farther up the mountain, Gussie picking his footsteps carefully, and staying a few paces behind the boss man, who edged forward with a fat stick smacking the ground on either side. And at the top of the slope they came to a ridge, a shinbone as it's called, along which they could walk on dry stony ground and view the lowlands of Roscommon to their right, and Mayo to their left.

'I pointed out Ballinasloe to him,' said Hughie. 'In the far distance. And I says, that's where your mammy is.'

They couldn't go any farther.

'But, Birdie, there wasn't a word out of him. Not a word.'

Not till they were back in the camp and starting on the whiskey and the tea sweetening their tongues.

'I wish I could tell you more,' says Hughie, 'but I can't. Not a word.'

2

THE GUARDS FILLED IN a few more details for her. The morning Gussie left the hospital, they said, he hitched a lift across the city to Salthill where he picked up the keys of an Opel Vectra. The property of Enda O'Driscoll, a beardy, blunt countryman who taught woodwork in a Galway vocational school, and who was happy to help an old schoolmate who was going through a bit of a rough patch. He had told Gussie on the phone the previous Monday that he could have the car for the two weeks, since he was going on holidays to the south of France on the following Saturday. He could pick up the keys that morning. Gussie reassured him that he would only need the car for a week. He intended finding another teaching job. And this time he believed that the loyalty of certain political friends of his father would pull strings.

Well, that was a consolation. To know he was back to himself. And they said that he was also intent on visiting Birdie. He was coming to her and he was going to bring her flowers or something. They said that. The O'Driscoll fellow claimed he spoke to him about it. About where to get flowers. But Birdie doesn't know what to believe sometimes. It can't all be true.

It was the stillness of the chestnut trees that morning which seemed to be holding up the sky. And it was a strange sky. Hughie said something like that.

A windless, grey stillness above the lake that was so potent, even the cry of the curlew conveyed the agony of Christ on His cross. The low ceiling of cloud, the colour of a mackerel's belly. The weather was so personal, Hughie said, that he felt its presence almost unbearable. As if the sky was looking at him.

He bid Gussie farewell, and then blessed himself and walked back up the lane to his house. He kept the dog at the range all day, for fear anything bad would happen him out in the world. The full canopy of chestnut leaf had fallen to the cobbles of the laneway. He even played a few slow tunes on the flute to placate the possible wrath of a divinity whose mercurial powers were beyond Hughie's intelligence, though not his instinct.

Poor Gussie. He was buoyant as he walked down the lane to the car. As if he had seen the light. As if it was a special day for him, to begin life again. Maybe it was the feeling of the steering wheel. The soft, rubbery leather. Or the smell of the car. That new car smell. Or maybe it was the airtight music of the CD player. But Gussie was in a bubble. A little bubble of his own happiness. That's what she'd like to believe. That's what Birdie would hope: that he was happy for once.

Driving through Athenry, he stopped for lunch and then for a drink in the hotel. The guards told her that. It was all recorded apparently. Sherlock fucken Holmes.

So he saw a truck from Quinn's quarry across the road filling up with petrol at the filling station. He saw drivers in the hotel restaurant sitting at the bar and eating their dinners in ravenous silence. They saw him and he saw them. He saw men in tracksuits standing in the corridor near the door of the leisure centre, waiting to go swimming. Or waiting for their wives. Or lovers.

He saw salesmen in the foyer flicking through glossy brochures of new cars, and fact sheets about life insurance spread on the coffee tables, as they waited for clients or regional managers or other people who made them nervous.

He may have seen the women in Tober going to Mass. But no, they weren't going to Mass. The guard said they were going to clean the church. And they saw him.

Well, that was good. That was almost like seeing him herself. Because Birdie knew some of those women. Women with sons. Women gathering all the secrets of their lives into thirty minutes of prayer at Mass every morning. Women remembering. Leafing through little-worn pages in their prayer books. Weddings and births and the moments of widowhood all measured out in holy pictures and anniversary cards. A sorrowful chorus in cheap headscarves. Old women dominated by young men who preached blather and poppycock with the confused hubris of medieval popes. Old women humbling themselves before some lizard in a clerical collar who blundered through the motions of Christ's death and Resurrection with the enthusiasm of a mechanic changing the plugs on a car engine. Don't talk! Birdie knew how women felt.

According to Hughie, Gussie was in good spirits when they parted company. Full of urgency to make amends. Get things back on track. Louise. He even mentioned Louise. Hughie said that.

And how many hours did Hughie and Birdie spend together, in the drawing room, when it was all over. Speculating on what was and what was not, as the evening closed in, the dark November evening, creeping up on them, unbeknownst.

They went as far as they could. That's where they went. They went as far as the facts would allow. But neither of them could really say with what excitement Gussie was contemplating his future, or how far out of the woods he had come. The thought of seeing him at her front door with a bunch of flowers was something that gave Birdie a pain in the chest. The prospect of him finding Louise again was another thing Birdie wasn't quite sure about. In short, neither Birdie nor Hughie nor the entire force of gardaí in every police station from Galway to Ballinasloe could really imagine what the hell he was thinking as he drove home to his mother. All anyone could do was accept that appointments with destiny are, by their nature, unexpected.

Gussie drove the new black Opel Vectra straight into the gable wall of Joyce's Spar shop on the outskirts of the village of Camlough. His body burst through the windscreen, but his legs got caught in the collapsed steering wheel, slamming his torso on to the bonnet of the car with a ferocity that smashed the face and the front lobe of his skull like an egg, breaking all the bones in his body, and in particular his backbone, which snapped clean in four places, destroying forever his spinal chord. Leaving him silent and immobile for what might remain of his life.

The mystery was that there were no flowers in evidence at the scene, though there was a porcelain dinner set on the passenger seat. Brightly coloured cups and saucers, and cheerful dinner plates and side plates, all painted in various blues. The box flew out the gap where the windscreen used to be a split second after Gussie. It flew like a cannonball, and exploded on the gable wall of the Spar shop with a soft whoosh that the entire village heard, and the street was drenched in china chippings as tiny as confetti. And could anyone give a satisfactory answer as to where that porcelain dinner set had come from? Or who owned it? Or did he buy it? And for what, or for whom? No. Nobody could answer that.

3

OH BIRDIE, BIRDIE, BIRDIE; you're an awful woman. The nurse said to read him letters. Tell him news of any special messages or of old friends who might call. Tell him everything. It would all help. The voices of old friends sometimes could have miraculous effects.

And you agreed. You phoned everyone you could. Relations. Friends. People in the school in Mullingar.

You went through his old books and copies in the room upstairs to see could you find old numbers. People he knew at school. People he knew at university. Anyone. Everyone. And for a day or two you even tried to talk to him yourself. But you couldn't bear his face.

So then you brought people to see him. And they told him the results of football matches and what they had been doing the previous night. Who they had a pint with. What colour the new wallpaper was. How much they had won on the scratch card. How cold it was on the bicycle that morning.

They told him that old Vincent Fagan was in with a brain tumour. Down the corridor. And that Tommy McCarthy was selling the garage. And Eddie Touhy was in as well. With thrombosis. And he had been put in the women's ward because of the overcrowding. Eddie! In with the women! Imagine that, they said. And the teacher in the school was being sued by the parents for sexual abuse and the headmaster had been suspended. But there wasn't a peep out of Gussie.

The local news was read out to him. Prayers were said in his ears. Scriptures were declaimed from the Bible.

The priest came and held his stiff sweaty hand. Pulled it up off the bedcovers and squeezed it. But there was no movement in the hot body or in the face that looked as if it had been run over by a tractor. The priest cajoled him. You'd swear Gussie was listening. He placed his hand on Gussie's forehead and pressed it. Then he sighed and looked at you, Birdie, with despair in his eyes. Despair that would have destroyed a pope. The nuns brought Padre Pio's glove. Relics for under the pillow. The nurses came every hour and changed him from one position to another. Promised a revolving bed as soon as one was free. They checked the tube that went down his throat, and shone little fountain-pen torches into his pupils, and stared at the monitor beside the bed that tracked his heartbeat, and signalled change in his temperature or blood pressure.

And all that time you sat there, Birdie! Sat in your little blue coat, with your black beret on your little grey head. Your tiny arthritic hands clasping your white, patent-leather handbag that contained the letter with the American stamp, which you couldn't bring yourself to open.

It came ten days after the crash. Someone must have told her. A story can go round the world as fast as round a village nowadays. But you couldn't open it. How could you open it? How could you read that? With all those people there. There was no telling what might be in a letter like that. So you deceived yourself, Birdie. You said you'd read it some other day. When things were quieter. Shame on you, Birdie!

You went home and left it on the dressing table in the bedroom. Discarded among the pills and jars of tablets and the ointments and face creams, and the antiseptic skin creams, and the scissors and combs and boxes of tissues.

You dropped it there, saying you'd bring it with you the following day when there was nobody about. But you didn't. You knew that the chaos of a dressing table would swallow it up. You'd never notice it again.

And what were you doing, Birdie? Just by the way. What were you doing on that day when your son hit the wall?

You were cleaning. What else?

Cleaning the cutlery in the kitchen drawer. That's where you found the scratch card, which he had sent the previous year for your birthday. The scratch card you never scratched. And so you took it out from under the forks and the knives, and you stared at it for a long time, wondering what it was. Then you remembered. And it annoyed you that he only thought it was worth his while to send you something as mean as a one-euro scratch card for your birthday. Is that all he thought about you? A scratch card!

– Hope you'll be lucky with this – the birthday card said.

A mean sort of present, you thought, at the time. And you threw it in the drawer, saying you'd scratch it later, but knowing full well that the chaos of the knives would swallow that too, and it would vanish beneath the forks and spoons and never be seen again.

Well, it was seen again. A day came for the scratch card to re-emerge. And what a day for it to come again!

But then you did sit down at the table in the kitchen and you scratched it with the end of a spoon and sure enough there were no matching numbers or signs. Worthless! Fucken worthless! says you.

And it was in that state of anxiety that you answered the hall door to a young guard, and a lady doctor who asked could they come in and sit down, and you didn't have to think for an instant. You didn't have to wonder for a second. No. You had been robbed again.

'It's Gussie, isn't it?' says you.

The policeman looked at the ground, but the young

lady doctor with rusty hair, all knitted into curls with some fancy shampoo, eyeballed you and said, 'Yes, Mrs Delaney, it's Gussie.'

Half an hour later you were sitting on the couch in the drawing room staring at the blank screen of the shrinking television and the lady doctor was pouring tea that the policeman had made.

Tea? Would you call it tea? It was tar you could paint the fence with! But say nothing. The poor young guard was happier in the kitchen and he was out of the way. The doctor did the talking. And you were saying how you had put up with a lot in life.

'Nobody knows the half of it,' says you.

You wept and the doctor looked at the ground, or her watch, and the policeman opened the door with a tray of rattling cups in his hands. Men can be so awkward sometimes. You stared at him, and for a minute you didn't know who he was or what he was doing there. And then you said, 'Guard, would you please for God's sake take off your hat when you're in the house!'

In the weeks that followed, you even enjoyed a measure of celebrity. Wasn't that nice? You were a person again. People spoke to you in the town when you took a taxi in to buy your yoghurt and bread and apples and oranges, and your few bits of meat in the supermarket. People phoned you. And they rang the bell every half-hour of the day. The house was never empty. You were losing a fortune on tea and biscuits. You were so exhausted, you had to ask people to leave.

But then after three weeks the doctors said that the tube was coming out. The machine was going off or something. The swelling in the face had gone down. You could recognize it as a human being. But not Gussie. Nobody could really tell who it was. A white porcelain face. He was in repose. Sleeping. And the doctors required her consent before turning him off. It would be a matter of a few days after that. A few weeks at the most.

Time to gather everybody, they said, but who was there to gather? And as you said to them, it would hardly matter to Gussie who was there. Yes, but it might matter to you, the man with the dicky bow said. You hadn't thought of that.

When he was off the machine for a few days, they moved him to the hospice. A harsh day of rain and wind. The ambulance driver helped the nurse with the stretcher. He was going to the same place where the Vet died. But the ambulance driver didn't know who the Vet was.

That's how it ended. You sitting there beside him. Some days. Any day you got a lift. And other days you stayed at home, sitting upstairs at the bedroom window, where you could see down the avenue. See who was coming and going.

Do you remember the time he broke your wedding present, Birdie? The lovely delph ornament: The Dancing Couple. The man in his tuxedo, and the lady in white, that twirled on the top of the wedding cake. None of your old cardboard shite. That was Belleek china. And he hammered the fucken thing to bits on the kitchen floor with the hammer from his Meccano set. Jesus, you were fit to be tied.

And black. And for some reason you said to him that if he didn't stop breaking things on you, then you'd have to throw yourself into the sea. Your dead body would go floating in the dark salty sea, and what would he do when that was dragged out? He'd be sorry then, wouldn't he? The poor little fellow screamed with fear. Oh yes, you had him to yourself that night. The Vet was out, like he always was, and no prospect of him home for hours. The old bottles of stout in the evenings didn't last long with the Vet, did they? No. So there you were accusing Gussie of scalding your heart, and sending him to bed without his supper. A long night that, Birdie, wasn't it? Staring at the old black-and-white television. Seeing nothing. Raging with yourself. Your body longing to touch him. Your body longing to enfold him for fuck's sake, and hold him, hold him, hold him, from the moment you closed his bedroom door.

You went to the spare bedroom that night because you had long lost your appetite for lying awake half the night beside the snoring Vet and him reeking of whiskey.

But now look at yourself, Birdie! You can touch him now. All you like. Your face is only an inch from his big empty moon of a face. You can hold him now all you fucken like.

No wonder you didn't want to go to the hospital after a while. No wonder you preferred sitting at home, on the bed upstairs, and staring down the long avenue at who was or was not coming or going.

Now if there are any messages, says the nurse, any letters, or little things out of the past that you could say to him, that would remind him of things, then you should try. Didn't she say that, Birdie? She did. You should try. But when you did come to visit him, you'd close the curtains and sit beside him, not a squeak out of either of you.

And now if there's any letters, Birdie, any letters, that you could read for him. Did you hear that, Birdie?

Oh yes you did. And you staggering from room to room, trying to recall his life, or find something that you could bring with you to show him. But there was nothing at all. The letter from America still lying on the bedroom dressing table. And the television in the drawing room downstairs still quietly shrinking.

LOUISE

I

BIRDIE THOUGHT it was lovely the way Louise appeared. Because someone like that is needed in a tragedy. Someone who is bright and cheerful, and who can take everybody's mind off the sad bits. And that's the way it was. There's no explaining it. These things just happen.

One moment Birdie is alone in the house trying to endure each day's new burden, and the next moment, behold, there's Louise, sitting across from her on the other armchair, large as life, organizing taxis, and phoning the hospital, and checking the fridge, and talking away about her life in America. She might as well have come from the moon. It would have made more sense to Birdie.

But at least Louise went out and had a life. No grass growing under that lady's feet. No locking herself in the wardrobe for fifteen years, or pacing beaches in the west of Ireland. Louise had been dancing in the American prairie. Isn't that what she said? Dancing with the wolf. A snow queen enfolded in dreams of the buffalo. Whatever that meant.

She had gone out for a summer fifteen years earlier, and then hung on for the winter to do an MA on Kit Carson and the Navajos of Arizona. And finally she stayed on in the university as a tutor and a minor lecturer in a place so cold and white that it was difficult to attract staff.

Where did she say it was? Somewhere in Minnesota? Or was it Montana? Anyway, wherever it was, they were delighted to have her.

They flew her in through snowstorms. Through Chicago. Through Minneapolis. And over long flat fields. A criss-cross of roads in the white wilderness. Granaries and cattle houses, and human dwellings in tiny clusters beneath the plane's wing. Their shining aluminium roofs glistening in the sunlight. And then she met a Chinaman.

No. She met a Colombian man in a Chinese restaurant. That was it. Someone called Charlie. Younger than her. And smaller too, no doubt. From Bogotá. But Louise asked no questions.

'I'd be the same in your position,' says Birdie. 'Ask no questions. It wasn't any of your business how he ended up in America. But go on anyway,' says Birdie.

And on Louise went, giving Birdie chapter and verse on her adventures since she had said goodbye to Ireland's shamrock shores fifteen years earlier. It was a distraction for Birdie. It cheered her up. It gave her some relief from that terrible hospice.

Louise condemned to scrubbing pots if you don't mind. Mopping floors. Gutting chickens. Clipping Chinese cabbages. Well, that was a long way from home.

'What made Milwaukee famous has made a loser out of me! Sure I had no money, Birdie. Not a penny, when I went out first.'

Birdie didn't know what made Milwaukee famous, and she couldn't understand why Louise kept repeating the same sentence. Some class of a joke over there, she supposed.

Charlie sometimes eyed her from the door of the kitchen, where he cooked large pots of soup in the afternoon, and prepared the meat for the stir-fry dishes. But he found time to help her out. Charlie could cut a dozen cabbages for her, and scrub ten pots. He was a salmon caught in her net.

It was difficult for Birdie to understand how she could claim to be happy in America. With all that skivvy work, as Birdie described it. And her with such a good education. To end up scrubbing pots! Couldn't get her head round that at all.

'Oh but, Birdie,' says she, 'the great thing was to be away from Ireland. To be sharing boiled rice in the back of the kitchen with a gorgeous boy from Colombia. To be away from Galway and Mullingar, and everywhere else.'

'I suppose,' said Birdie.

'I couldn't breathe in Ireland. I told him that.'

I suppose.

'Do you know what I'm going to tell you, Birdie girl? Do you know the history of Ireland is the history of transport?'

Now how did she make that out?

'Well,' says she, 'in the beginning was the horse. Am I right?'

OK.

'And then there was the bicycle. And then there was the cars. Cortinas. Austin 1100s. Ford Anglias. Datsun Cherrys. And eventually they invented the Airbus, and the green card, and the European passport, and the world was our oyster.'

'Some of us,' Birdie said with a grin. 'Some of us.'

Charlie from Colombia had two jobs. He cooked in the restaurant during the day, and at night he was an electrician in the local radio station. And Louise had two lives as well. Studying in the university library half the week, and cutting cabbages in a restaurant for the other half. With her lovely man. From China. Or Colombia.

And what was he like, Louise?

'Well, he was a little wiry fellow, Birdie. Would you believe that? With beautiful dark eyes. But not tall. No. When we were standing beside each other, he only came up to me chest. Me breastbone! And he'd say – Dizz eez crazee!"'

Goodness!

Charlie had a big broad smile and he spoke in little gusts of breath because he was shy about his poor English.

When they finished cutting chickens and chopping cabbages for the weekend, Charlie and Louise would sit on high stools, flicking dollars on the counter, drinking beer and reflecting on the fact that booze was the curse of the Irish.

'Oh now, that's the truth,' says Birdie.

'Because people had nothing better to do,' says Louise, 'and because they didn't get off this little island, and most Irish people don't have a clue what is going on in the big world. They don't open the door and look outside. Do they, Birdie?'

'No. You're right there now, Louise. They do not.'

Charlie and Louise flicking more dollars on the counter. Ten- and twenty-dollar bills as they became more pissed.

'Pissed, Birdie. You don't mind the language.'

Oh not at all.

'Pissed!'

The bar packing up with young people and U2 blaring from the jukebox.

'Oh yes. The electric coal scuttle as the Vet used to call it. Dear oh dear. That's not today or yesterday. But go on!'

Charlie and Louise are out on the town. Charlie twirls on his high stool to view the crush of young women in leather jackets and Louise twirls too, and gazes at the strong boys in sleeveless tee shirts and tank tops.

Two drunks walking down College Drive towards the river at midnight. Everyone knows they are lovers, the way they link arms, and stop every so often to hug and kiss and wag fingers at each other with profound advice, or sing together their favourite song.

'What made Milwaukee famous has made a loser out of me!'

That was the way. Off down the alley, waving goodnight to the policeman in his car by the kerb, their hands high in the air.

'Such a picture!' said Birdie.

'Oh such a life, Birdie!' said Louise. 'Such a life!'

2

LOUISE WAS SICK, the day she heard the news, lying in bed all day nursing a hangover. She cooked eggs, ham waffles and syrup. She thought the feed would put her stomach right. It usually did. And then she slept for most of the day. Charlie kept to his side of the bed until noon, watching the television. Then he got up.

A few neighbours came in. Friends of Charlie. They all sat in the kitchen brewing coffee and talking about the ice. Charlie kept complaining about welfare.

'All these guys on the reservation! They get welfare,' he says. 'But me. I get nothing. Nothing at all.'

Then he started giving off about Europe. She shouted at him to shut up. He was like a radio. Sometimes you had to turn him off. Anyway, he came back to bed in the afternoon, and played with the TV remote control for a while, flicking from CNN to the local channels every few seconds. And then he wanted to talk. Something on the news had caught his attention, but she was still trying to sleep. He said a woman in Alberta had left a baby alone with a Dobermann pinscher, and when she came back, the baby was in shreds. Louise said she couldn't care less. She wanted to sleep.

'So later the police come and they want to shoot the dog. And what does she do?'

'I don't know what she does,' says Louise, exasperated. She was trying to sleep.

'She takes a case against them,' says Charlie, 'for shooting the dog. She tells the judge: a baby I can make any time, but that dog cost me five hundred dollars.'

Louise didn't believe him but she said nothing. She knew he exaggerated stories just to get her attention. And she remembered it all in such detail because it was just then that she got the phone call from a friend in Ireland, a girl who had been in her class, who said she just wanted to say that she heard Gussie's name on the television. He was in a road accident or something, and he's badly injured, but he's going to be OK.

'Well, I was gobsmacked, Birdie,' says Louise. 'Gobsmacked.'

Charlie said he might go ice-fishing on the Sunday morning, and she said sure, because they lived sort of separate lives anyway, when it all came down to brass tacks.

After a while he paid attention only to the television.

And during the day, while she was at the university, he would be down in the basement smoking dope.

That night they went to another dinner party, and Louise was sitting beside a woman called Mary, who had curly hair and talked to Charlie all the time if you don't mind, and said her grandparents were from Ballywhooly. So then Louise said to Charlie that she wasn't in good form. And maybe she still had the hangover. And so she decided to go home in a taxi and leave Charlie at the mercy of the Rose of Ballywhooly with the twinkling eyes.

To be fair to Charlie, he offered to go with her, but she wouldn't dream of taking him away from his new friend. Maybe Louise was thinking of Gussie. He was in the back of her mind. So she left the party. But not before kissing Charlie on the mouth. That might induce the curly girl whose mammy came from Ballywhooly as a war bride, to pause for thought, before leaping on someone else's property.

'Of course!'

And on the way home that night she kept thinking of the sky and looking up into it. It was so full of stars now. And sometimes in Montana, or Milwaukee, or wherever it was, sometimes the sky there can be bigger than anything else.

3

WELL, THERE WAS ONLY ONE message on her answering machine. It was from her brother in Tuam. He wanted to know what was the name of her boyfriend when she was at college, because, says he, he heard some name on the television that sounded fierce like him. She clicked the

machine off and went in to the loo and she was there thinking of Gussie, and would you believe, she fell asleep on the
loo seat. Ah now, isn't that awful! But anyway. There was no
sign of her Colombian lover-boy returning the following
morning, or even all day Sunday.

So that evening she went out again. This time on her
own. What a social life! There was a dinner for members
of the faculty club. Harry was there from the Art Department. The dandruff man who had known Rolf Harris years
ago. And the boss of the department, a small, frightened
man, grey-haired, with a knack of concentrating too hard
on everything she was saying, so that she knew he was
always thinking filthy thoughts. There was a novelist from
Belgium who was teaching a creative writing programme.
There was Walter, the old actor with the cravat. And a Cali-
fornian specialist on Focault with two new hips.

Two! Not just one? No, two.

Fuko?

Pardon!

Fuko?

A philosopher.

Oh.

And apparently Louise got drunk and played the pan
pipes very badly. The actor did too many party pieces from
Elizabeth Bishop's poetry, and Louise was so knackered
that she hardly remembered going home in the taxi. But
she couldn't sleep.

'Of course not.'

So an hour later she was stumbling around the kitchen,
drinking hot chocolate, and singing Christy Moore songs,
because in that hungover condition she always felt fragile. Walking around the kitchen, sipping hot drinks and

singing the Planxty songs from years ago was, usually, the solution. It filled a gap. But she felt silly. And it was four in the morning, and there was no sign of the man who was supposed to have gone ice-fishing for the weekend. She was thinking to herself that it was more like an ass hole than an ice hole he'd be fishing in, at that hour of a Sunday night or Monday morning.

'Sorry, Birdie! Sorry! It just came out.'

And that's when she wrote the letter.

'Oh yes,' says Birdie, 'the letter.'

That is when she sat down at the coffee table in the living room and folded open an A4 jotter that she used for making all sorts of notes and doodles on, and she took a pen from the notepad beside the phone, and she wrote that letter to Gussie.

And the things that poured out!

'I read over it immediately and I couldn't believe it, Birdie. I couldn't believe it.'

I suppose.

'I mean it was a love letter. You know that, Birdie. Things I never realized were inside me. It was a love letter, Birdie.'

'Oh. I see.'

The more she wrote, the more the pen shook in her hand. She was shivering, even though all the central heating was on and the stove was lit, and she was wearing her pyjamas, and a big jumper, underneath a fleece dressing gown.

'I was astonished,' says Louise. 'I knew I had to come home and see him.'

Astonished! Birdie was astonished as well, thinking of the letter lying unopened, upstairs on the dressing table.

COMPANIONS

I

THERE WERE TIMES during those weeks when Birdie thought of only one person. Of nothing else and nobody else. But it wasn't Gussie. Birdie went to sleep at night whispering his name. And she woke sometimes smiling at the thought of him. Hughie Donoghue. Hubert. Mr Donoghue. Dattledo. Not that many would remember his nickname now.

And during those weeks when Gussie was sleeping his big coma in the hospice, Birdie's heart was as unfamiliar to her as a land on which snow had fallen. She was so confused that she left everything to Hughie.

Hughie formed all her opinions for her; he made all her decisions. Birdie just listened to him. Soaked him in. She was like blotting paper. She would have been an imbecile without him. He was her staff.

And in her mind she was assembling a detailed picture of her Hughie. Assembling his life from every random detail she could pick up. From all the queries she had for him, about what he ate for breakfast and had he ever fixed up the old cottage with the galvanized roof. Knitting together all the accidental details that dropped from his mouth, until at last, there it was – a perfect tapestry. Her very own private Hughie.

She sees him first thing in the morning. Washing his face in a bucket by the range, which he has lit long before dawn. She sees a shirt, a vest and underpants hanging above the range, all still slightly damp.

What can you say about men? They never change. She sees him soaping his body as he stands on the flags and then taking a kettle from the range, and pouring it into the bucket to heat what is there, and then he rinses himself with a warm damp cloth. From beneath the sofa the dog watches the ritual with cautious curiosity.

Hughie, preparing himself to visit her. Preparing for his pilgrimage. Like a monk doing his beads or his chores, or his ritual practice, Hughie gets up every morning and washes himself, and then steps out into the world, on his way to her.

There are three rooms in Hughie's cottage: the kitchen and two bedrooms, one to the west of the kitchen, and one to the east. The room east of the kitchen is only a storeroom now, cluttered with years of abandoned junk. The mangle and the hames and the holy pictures. The trunks that came from America decades ago. The tilly lamps. The old rocking chair with no back. A tongs for the fire. The remains of a bed. And a thousand other small boxes of wires, plugs, old clocks, broken vases and copies of religious magazines his mother used to read a very long time ago.

Hughie rummages and burrows and pokes for half an hour before he finds the iron in there. Then he makes it operational on the kitchen table, where he presses his white shirt, and his green tie, and the trousers of his brown television suit.

Men.

By then the underclothes are dry and, with huffs and puffs and blistering curses, he negotiates his withered old bones into the vest and the long johns, and into the shirt and the suit. He's not as bronze as he once was. In fact, he has turned very white. And thin.

Birdie can imagine him stretched in his coffin but she dispels that terrible image.

Once Hughie puts on the suit, the RTÉ suit he once wore into the studios to make the music programme, and which fits him better now than it did then, he is a changed man. He is back to the old style. The old Dattledo.

Men never know what to do with their hair. Birdie chastised him about that. It was too long. It gave him the gimp of a clown. He confessed to her once that he manicured himself every Saturday night with the same fastidious attention as when he was a young lad. Brightening his locks to a garish rusty brown with dollops of henna, and combing it with the latest Brylcreem available in Tiernan's chemist's shop in Crosshill. A waste of money, she told him. It's having no effect. 'Go to the barber and get a haircut. It's not hygienic. At your age.'

But an old man's vanity is like a rope. They think that if they let go, they'll fall off the cliff.

Ten times he'd comb that hair before he left the house. Putting the last details to the ears with a comb in front of the saucer-sized mirror, which hung on a nail beside the door. His mother had put it there when he was a child. And ten more times he'd comb it again and rearrange it in the taxi. And a further ten times upstairs in Birdie's bathroom.

'Arah, Hughie, will you for God's sake come down, or we'll be late.'

'Patience, patience, patience,' says he to her one day, 'the hair must be combed.'

'Yes,' she says, 'but why do I have to endure it?'

'Oh Missus Delaney,' says he, 'you above all people should know that life is hard but it must be endured.'

'Do you think so?'

They were in the back of the taxi. Whizzing along the suburbs towards the hospice.

'My dog does be whingeing when I put on the suit in the mornings, for he does know that whenever I comb me hair at the mirror and put on the suit, it signifies that he'll be chained to the wall of the cowshed for the majority of the day. I know that whine. I acknowledge it and I do say this to him: Shep, I do say, life is hard, but it must be endured.'

The taxi driver was eyeing them through the rear-view mirror. 'Oh now,' says he, 'that's quare fucken true.'

And just like on the steps of that posh hotel in Killarney, with all the gardens, Hughie winks at her. And he laughs a chesty smoker's laugh, as he holds open the door of the taxi for her. He links arms with her and escorts her up the stone steps, and he opens for her the big glass door into the hospice foyer. That's the style of him.

2

'OH, I DIDN'T KNOW you came so far,' she said to Louise. Apparently Louise got stuck in the airport in Minneapolis or somewhere, and wondered would she make her connection. Chicago it was. Yes. She had to come through Chicago. And the flight was delayed for an hour. So she phoned someone called Tania, and then had a roast beef bagel, with sesame and potato salad.

'Must have been lovely.'

She sat down on this seat. An end seat in a row of blue plastic seats, across from the signs for gates 9 and 10 and the desks for Northwest. Gates? Just a word, Birdie. It's where you queue up for the flight. In the airport.

'Oh.'

Anyway. People were reading newspapers, staring at their laptops, and watching the football on the television. One lady in a fur coat with blonde hair was drinking from a bottle of vodka. And there was a row of ten cubicles with telephones, and all these men in suits had their computers plugged in and they were all typing messages on their machines like a factory of sewing-machine operators.

'Then what happened?'

Well. Louise was just sitting there, daydreaming, and her eyes jumping from one place to the next, and taking in everything and taking in nothing. Passing the time.

'Right.'

Because in the years she had been in Montana or Colorado, or wherever it was, she had been back to Ireland only twice. Once to see her brother's new house in Athenry, and once to attend the First Holy Communion of her sister's daughter, Angela.

It was a long journey.

'Of course. You were very good to come,' says Birdie.

In the airport Louise was looking at everything but seeing nothing. She was in a dream of snow. A universe of snow. Lost in an infinity of snow. And then it was 7.45, and she noticed that Flight 144 had vanished from the board.

'And was that bad?'

Oh, that was bad alright. She had to run as fast as she could to catch flight 142, which was six gates away.

'Goodness!'

And she cursed all the way. Her rucksack flopping on her back and bumping against people as she flew through them. Well, that was terrible. But she got there.

'You got home?'

No. She got as far as Chicago.

'Chicago? That's a long way off.'

Yes. And then Yuri met her at the airport.

'Yuri?'

A Russian professor. Well, Louise seems to know people everywhere. Marvellous. And Yuri had fleshy jowls, and a cheap, brown leather jacket and matching leather gloves.

'And his mouth was enormous, Birdie. The lips, teeth and jaws of a donkey. And he talked about Shakespeare, and how one must read plays on the flow of the metre rather than by the meaning of the line, which he said is the mistake the English make!'

Louise couldn't follow him. And Birdie couldn't follow Louise either. But Louise was glad to meet Natasha.

Who was Natasha?

Yuri's girlfriend.

'Of course.'

They had both agreed to let Louise stay overnight because, you see, what with the flight from Mississippi or wherever, and it being late, well, Louise couldn't get her Dublin flight until the following day. And apparently Yuri's exotic lips, which pressed against her cheek in a flirtatious kiss, made her pity everyone who spent all their money on big bungalows in east Galway.

'I'm not quite with you, Louise,' says Birdie.

'He was romantic, Birdie. That was the point. Lord, Yuri was dangerous. If you found yourself alone with him.'

'And as Natasha said, it's not just his lips that were like the donkey. Oh Jesus, Birdie! I'm terribly sorry.'

Sorry for what, Birdie wanted to know. Sure there was nothing to be sorry about. Birdie was only delighted to be as far away as possible from Gussie's bed, and from all the lime-green curtains of the hospice ward, which sheltered the dying from each other, when they wanted moments of privacy with their families. Birdie was only too happy to be transported into Natasha's life in Chicago with its amber jewellery and the large, green, frog cushion on the bed. The wooden floors. The giant television. An orange parrot in a cage. A bicycle in the hall. Bananas hanging from a blue string over the wooden kitchen table. Pink carnations in a vase over the cooker. And Yuri's room where Natasha was sleeping, with the Star Wars duvet. The big open world of an American apartment.

3

AND IN THE OLD DAYS you could get a lift anywhere. Stand on the side of the road. Listen to the sound of a motorcar far off in the distance. And then it came closer. And there was rarely a time when a car didn't stop.

'There wasn't as many cars as now. No. But you see, Birdie, in another way it was better, 'cos more of them stopped. Are you with me?' Hughie asked.

Oh, she was with him all right.

'And when I got into the passenger seat I would offer

the driver a cigarette and he would take one and we'd talk about where he was from and where he was going, and where I was from and so on.

'The weather was analysed. The morning news was recited. And eventually I would put my view, my entire philosophy of life, on the table. The driver listened. He considered. And then he might offer me a smoke. Now this was a great education, if you think about it. For I tended to rehearse a different world view in each car. And I'd suit my philosophy to what I could guess about the driver's face.

'And I could always tell if the driver was enjoying himself, because he would begin to drive slow, and he'd start waving his hand at all the other cars we'd meet. All the men and women on the roadside, and you know this yourself, Birdie; in those days they would be cutting hedges, or wheeling barrows of dung, or sitting on tractors smoking their own cigarettes, and they would always wave at a passing car. They'd put their arms up and their hands high in the air, as if welcoming the homecoming troops from a far-off adventure.

'And no matter where I was in Ireland – and this is the truth, Birdie – there was always a pub within five miles that had great music. Are you with me? And Guinness. A place where the landlady would make the stars dance on the back of her hand, and never let a musician leave her house hungry without a few sandwiches cut as thick as doorsteps, and big salty slices of a recently boiled rump of bacon.

'Oh Jaysus, Birdie, them were the days.

'So before I knew where I was, the smell of drink was wafting up me nose, and I was leaning on the counter, talking poetry and playing reels and I'd forget where I was going, or who I was with, or how I was ever going to get home to the dog and the old broken-down chair in that derelict cottage me poor mother died in. God rest her soul.'

'God rest her soul,' says Birdie.

4

AND WHERE WOULD they be without Tommy Smith? That's what Birdie wondered during those weeks. Where would they be without Tommy going out of his way to taxi them here, there and yonder, and God knows did he ever take a penny for his trouble?

Tommy was a recovered alcoholic who came from Cavan to study something at the university years ago, until the booze and the Galway air sank him without a trace. Then, as if in another life, he re-emerged as a taxi driver in Crosshill. Always happy to oblige Hughie.

Hughie, for some reason, was his favourite customer. He was half the height of Hughie. And half his age. A little potbelly on him, and a black moustache and a bush of black hair. Birdie reckoned that he must have been using the wrong shampoo. There was far too much body in his thatch, so that it looked like a helmet. But men can be told nothing, so Birdie sang dumb.

He was Hughie's friend. He'd collect Hughie from the cottage.

'Is it Galway you're heading for?' he'd inquire through the rear-view mirror. The same question was posed every day.

'That's correct,' Hughie would say.

And that was the end of conversation until they passed Mountbellew.

'Not a bad morning,' Hughie conjectured.

'It's not,' agreed Tommy. 'But will it fucken last?'

Through Menlough and Monivea Hughie knew where he was, but coming into the city, he could hardly recognize the roads, and the motorways that had been rolled through hills and valleys and swamps and woodlands, flattening all before them.

The fields were dotted with mansions. Two-storey buildings with double oak doors like castles, and ten windows to each façade, with garages as big as small cottages, and long, tarred driveways through green lapis-lazuli lawns. All landscaped with the same Norwegian maples and Himalayan birches.

'Not a sign of a cow,' Hughie said to the taxi man.

'No fucken loss,' says Tommy.

'And those gardens. You could play billiards on them.'

'Aye, but where's the fucken money to pay for them. That's the point.'

'I mind a time,' Hughie said, 'when those little fields were nothing but daisies.'

'Ah but look, it's a quare fucken road now, eh?'

Then Tommy put his foot down, pressing the pedal to the floor like a man for whom bypasses and four-lane motorways and roundabouts were second nature. Hughie slipped him a twenty-euro note at the hospice door, and Tommy manoeuvred his torso like a sack of potatoes to face Hughie in the back seat.

'Now I know what's going on in there, Hughie. Right? And I want you to know I'm here, Hubert. D'ya understand me now? For you and the lady. Right? I'm fucken here, Hubert. OK? Day or night, Hubert. Day or night!'

GUSSIE

I

YOU COULD SAY he was famous for a day. Just after the crash. He was discussed on the radio and the television. The mangled Vectra was plastered all over the following morning's newspaper. A photograph of Gussie on the basketball court in Kinnegad, smiling innocently at the camera with a sports whistle hanging on a string around his neck, and teenage girls in sports gear hopping the ball and making funny faces to the camera. He was a school teacher. That's what the papers said. Nothing about the fact that he had been off work for over a year.

Not that the fame lasted long. His catatonic state in the hospice was of no interest to the nation. Not much of a story there. Even by the time Louise appeared on the scene, the national interest had moved elsewhere.

At that time Gussie was still in the regional hospital. And she arrived one day out of the blue, and she was told that the doctors were still doing their rounds in the ICU, and so she strolled across the foyer and bought a copy of *The Irish Times* in the kiosk that sold flowers and chocolates and she sat at the window to read it. But what she didn't realize at the time was that the tall man sitting beside her, flicking through the *Connaught Tribune*, was the legendary flute player Dattledo Donoghue.

There they were, the pair of them, for the first time, sitting beside each other, engrossed in their respective papers.

And there was lots of news for both of them. Consternation in Limerick, apparently, at the mysterious death of a cow. And special provision being made by the Department of Education for children who were diagnosed with Attention Deficit Disorder, which the paper described as a new phenomenon in Ireland.

Louise tried to push herself through it. Page after page. Soaking up the local stories, with the ravenous curiosity of someone just off the plane. And there was a story about wine drinkers. Another new phenomenon. And suntan lotions that might be toxic. And promises of a vaccine for HIV.

– There was a time and it wasn't too far back, she read, when the plain people of Ireland had crude and unrefined palates. –

Really?

– But all that has changed. There is now official confirmation that the country has transmogrified into a snazzy and urbane land chock-full of Chardonnay-quaffing sophisticates. –

Well, aren't we just wonderful?

In short, there wasn't much happening in Ireland in the week that Gussie hit the wall. Now if he had hit the Spar shop on the same day as a bomb in Belfast maybe, or a rocket attack on Manhattan, or an earthquake in Asia, or a building falling down in South America, he might not have made it to the front page. No. He might have been stuffed into the middle bits.

So if Gussie was looking for fame, then he picked the right week to hit the wall, and he had achieved his goal. Not that Gussie was looking to be famous. That's about the last thing in the world poor Gussie wanted. Drawing attention to himself. But he certainly managed to draw attention to himself in the end.

Louise was too jet-lagged for the amount of anxiety that was in the daily newspaper, so she went to find a coffee machine. Hughie, on the other hand, was chuckling his way through the regional paper, like a scooter eating up a motorway. A tonic he called it. A cure for all melancholies and depressions.

'Just read the court cases in the local paper and you'd fall around laughing.'

He read it from cover to cover every Friday.

Then the pair of them got the call that the ICU was open to visitors, and they both walked down the long corridor lined with empty trolleys and incubators and heart machines. Past the Surgical and the Medical wards. Asking directions at the stations along the way. And eventually, arriving at the ICU, holding their breath on the threshold, and then, and only then, realizing that they were both heading for the same bed.

There before them, lying rigid and still, and protected by two cot-sides was the unfortunate Gussie, an enormous green plastic tube stuffed down his throat. Lines for drips and urine bags needled into his arms. His head was so crisscrossed with stitching that it reminded Hughie of a football. Louise thought he looked as serene as a sleeping baby. But it affected her. It did. Louise had to sit down almost immediately. She just burst out suddenly. Very dramatic and loud. Rocking herself in the chair and whining. Oh, she never expected it would have that effect. She really was shocked. And that at least hid the fact that Hughie's hands were trembling, and that he was having no success in his attempts to get the handkerchief out of his trouser pocket and clear his eyes.

2

AND WHERE WERE YOU, BIRDIE?

At home. Isn't that right? Yes. Sitting in your drawing room, with your back glued to the armchair, and your two hands gripping either armrest. The fingers of your right hand tapping away like an impatient detective. Tapping out something from Wagner maybe. Isn't that the fellow the Vet used to play? That dark chocolate-in-the-river music. Tapping away the time because you knew even this would pass.

This waiting.

Everything passes. The Vet playing his records. He passed. You and him dancing. Oh that surely passed, didn't it?

Whoosh.

Remember the day after he died, when you first poked out the old records from their sleeves and you clipped one of them onto the silver rod inside the gramophone and waited to hear Karajan conduct the Berlin Philharmonic. That was the stuff to waken the dead. And all that passed. Everything. If you sit long enough, everything dissolves.

Life is about endurance. No matter who is behind the curtain. The one sure fact is that if you sit it out, they'll go away.

So you sat, Birdie, for hours, and days, and then weeks.

Staring at the curtain. You had been sitting since the Vet died. Sitting since they took little Momo away in her tiny white coffin. And of course there's no point denying that there have been times in recent years when you missed sex; when you regretted that all that messy stuff was gone forever.

The Vet never spoke of it. He just executed the operation with the rhythm of a man who saw animals doing it in farmyards day in and day out. He knocked on your door when he wanted it. And then he'd enter your darkness with an exquisite lack of romance, which caused you to shiver and tingle. Strangely enough, the delight was more intense than if he had come reciting the collected poems of Pablo Neruda. But you wouldn't have objected to a little bit of conversation as well. A little bit of Pablo Neruda. That was the book Louise gave Gussie the Christmas before they parted. What was it called? *The Captain's Verses*. Nice poems. But a fat lot of good it did poor Gussie. Louise may have hoped it was a road map that Gussie might follow.

And there you are again! Back to Gussie. Everything comes back to Gussie. No matter how you try to be elsewhere. Gussie, who couldn't read road maps. Couldn't even watch the fucken road.

Your liberation was a washing machine. No. Before that, it was a cooker. The first year you were married. Remember the cooker? A magnificent electric cooker that cost five pounds. Five pounds. That was liberation.

And it was only when you were fifty that the thought occurred to you that there was nothing mechanically, physically or theologically wrong with women driving cars.

Of course the Vet couldn't understand your point, though it didn't bother him, and eventually you found a retired district nurse to teach you.

She gave you one lesson, during which you forgot to close the door and almost fell out of the car. But there was no stopping you after that. You went to the golf club and left the Vet (who was by then retired) to look after himself for the afternoon. That is to say that when you had served him his dinner at one o'clock, and washed up the dishes, you put an egg in the egg saucepan and left it on the cooker with a note saying not to forget the water. You left buttered bread on a plate, and two spoons of loose tea in the pot.

That was liberation.

So yes, Birdie, yes! You sailed into old age as a lady of leisure. Liberated enough to play a round of golf with Mrs MacDermody, who had a foghorn voice on the fairways and smoked forty Sweet Afton a day and denounced women who work on the wireless as a pack of cunts.

One day the wireless women claimed that young girls nowadays have better chances and more opportunities than in the old days. And they do, no matter what Mrs MacDermody feels in her bitter old heart.

'It's definitely true,' you said. 'The young ones nowadays have a far better chance.'

'A better chance at what?' sneered Maura MacDermody and then she went on to answer her own question in a thunderous voice, and her old rotten breath like a dragon's coming out of her cancerous lungs. You were only afraid the Reverend Tompkins would hear her, for he was just ahead of you, near the ninth green.

'Well, to hear you talking,' says MacDermody, 'you think that women in my day were a crowd of fucken eejits pissing holy water.'

All Birdie said was that she thought young women nowadays were getting a better chance.

'A better chance at what? A better chance to make the likes of you and me out to be gobshites because we went through life without a fucken job. We never needed jobs. Didn't we have husbands?'

She bellowed like an old rhinoceros, and then she belted the ball straight across the ninth fairway, as far as the next green, nearly knocking the head off the reverend clergyman, who had to duck, before she replaced her driver in the bag as if she was returning a sword to its scabbard.

'Fucken cunts!'

But she's dead now, Birdie. She doesn't be talking like that now, does she? And she did use that language. But not any more. No. You were at the funeral. And that's years ago. How many years ago is it? Oh, very hard to say that. And you're still there, Birdie. Still tapping your fingers. Passing the time. Waiting for *Coronation Street*.

3

HUGHIE WAS THE FIRST to visit her. His hair oiled like the axle of a cart, and combed in straight lines. His fingers agitated in his trouser pockets, and his shoe tapping the ground as he stood, hoping Birdie wasn't at home, or that she might not hear the bell. After walking up the drive, he now regretted his sudden rush of compassion.

Birdie opened the door.

'Long time, Mrs Delaney,' says he. 'Long time. How are ye?'

She was dumbstruck.

'I was in the hospital on Tuesday,' he said. 'For tablets.

There's a clinic on Tuesdays. For the nerves. And I seen the child in the queue. He must be going through a bit of stormy weather.'

That was the day the pair of them decided to visit Gussie in the psychiatric ward. Neither of them knew what was coming.

Birdie felt weak when she saw his withered features at the door, but she let him in, and sat him down in the front room before saying anything. They sat for two hours in the armchairs opposite each other, with an electric heater drying the air to an unbearable tightness, and the light slowly fading from the sky. Before he left, it was twilight. The hour between the dog and the wolf, as Hughie used to call it.

Only when he said he'd go did she comment on the fading day, and he got up to flick the light switch. The moment he switched on the light, he could see his reflection in the window. It was that dark.

He said he heard that Gussie was going through a bit of stormy weather. Said he'd be glad to go into the psychiatric ward with her, if she needed support. Said he knew that place like the back of his hand. A bit of a stormy patch. But he'd be out in a week.

Birdie had enormous loyalty to the Vet, and she rarely pictured him lying in the cold clay of the old graveyard.

Instead, she sometimes imagined him standing under the trees near the church door, where he had waited for her all those years before, when she came on her father's arm to marry him. And she was a long time staring at the electric fire, thinking to herself how Hughie had a terrible rim of dirt round his neck, and how he must have no comforts at all in that old cottage he lived in. But she didn't dare say much.

'You were great on the flute,' says she.

He said he hadn't played it for years. He was leaning back in the chair and stretching his legs so that he seemed very comfortable there. And it was nice to have someone to talk to for the evening. Especially with Gussie in the psychiatric ward. And both of them tried to sustain the moment as long as possible.

They agreed to go the following morning to the hospital to see the patient. Hughie said he'd come in a taxi and they'd share the cost, but Birdie insisted she'd pay the entire bill. Then he left.

'Mind yourself on the avenue,' says she when he was on the doorstep. 'There's no light down there.'

And that was the beginning of it. Eight weeks ago. Whoosh.

4

IT WAS ABOUT TWO WEEKS after the accident when Louise appeared. Gussie was still in the hospital on the machine. She came to the door with a bunch of flowers, and broke down in tears, as if she had been Gussie's wife or something.

Birdie examined her face for wrinkles or touches of salt in the hair, and Louise wiped her eyes and then tried to be cheerful and make up things about Montana, and she went through a litany of what her brothers and sisters did and where they lived, and how many children they all had, and the cost of bungalows in Galway. She said she didn't really know him that well.

'Of course you didn't,' says Birdie. 'The pair of ye were just kids.'

And then Louise told her about the letter and Charlie and all that. And Birdie said she had something upstairs. She went edging her way out the door and up the stairs, one at a time and Louise could hear her in the bedroom above, fumbling about, hitting the wardrobe, dropping her walking stick, and eventually the same slow procedure in reverse, until Birdie was again at the foot of the stairs, and out of breath. Her lips were blue. In her hand she had the unopened letter.

'I couldn't read it to him,' she said. 'I can't even go and look at him.'

Louise fixed all that. At the foot of the stairs.

'Will you bring me in?' says Birdie.

Louise said of course she would. So Louise came the following day again, and this time with Hughie and Tommy Smith.

'Don't we all have troubles, Mrs Delaney?' says Tommy. 'It comes to everyone's door but I'm here, Mrs Delaney. I'm here. Day or night now. I want you to understand that. Day or night.'

Well, that was a big step, wasn't it? And, after that, Louise and Hughie became her constant companions. Her support and staff. And that was a great help. She cried her way from the door of the hospital all the way to his bed. Birdie was no joke when it came to tears. When the floodgates opened.

Down the long corridor, through the Medical and Surgical units, crying deeper and with greater disturbance the closer she got. Sometimes it would subside and then her eye would light on a trolley or a respirator or an incubator, and those mechanical objects had a powerful effect on her. Away she'd go again into the floods.

Hughie and Louise flanked her. Even Tommy took up the rear. He couldn't resist it. And the procession drew the attention of doctors and nurses and other visitors on their way to see relatives and friends in the wards. A procession of sorrow. That's what it was. And eventually Birdie's dry, blotting-paper face, crowned with a tiny feathery hat, could make no more tears, could construct no more expressions. Not even glances of comprehension.

Birdie could cry no more. She was an empty mask. A false face. An existential uncertainty that wobbled along the corridor and impelled doctors to ask the ward sisters who might that person be who was passing amongst them.

She reached the bed, and there, leaning on her stick, she trembled and tried to take a hankie from her coat pocket, which would not come out and she became completely involved in the attempt until Louise pulled it out for her and gave it to her so that she could blow her nose. Birdie had nothing left.

'Gussie,' she said. Leaning on her stick at the foot of the bed. 'Gussie.'

Then she moved to the side of the bed and sat down, and her face looked up at the ceiling and it contorted in a grotesque and silent screech.

Other extraordinary things happened in the days and weeks that followed. Louise read him the letter. That was a moment that took Birdie's breath away. They were all listening. Birdie and Hughie and some woman in a dressing gown who used to wander in from the female ward every so often to see if there was anything she could do.

And later that night in a fancy hotel on the outskirts of the town, Louise, throwing caution to the wind, and having nowhere to go with the emotion which that letter had released in her, permitted Hughie to unzip her jeans and loosen the clips of her bra and slobber all over her. A man with old withered hands. A man with white, wrinkled flesh as cold as marble. Sweet Divine Jesus, the fucken hussy! His rotten breath already smelling of the grave.

The next day Birdie asked her. Straight out. 'In the name of Christ,' says Birdie, as if for a moment she was Louise's mother, 'what did you think you were doing last night?'

5

THERE WAS A SMELL of sausages and rashers in the hospice on the evening Gussie was admitted. It was teatime and the whole place felt cozy and homely. Gussie was in a ward, but it didn't feel like a ward. Each bed was curtained on three sides. They were more like cubicles. And there was plenty of distance between one bed and the next. There were pretty little lamps in different pastel colours on the pedestals beside each bed.

On one side of Gussie's bed, there was a beautiful young woman, wasted to a skeleton by the ravages of cancer. It was her last few days on earth. She was waiting for the inevitable, she said. And because her daughter was out having chips in McDonald's and Gussie wasn't talking to anyone, Birdie found herself chatting to this beautiful woman, who told her she wasn't afraid to die, with eyes so intense and wide that Birdie knew she was scared out of her wits, but just couldn't admit it.

She was a bright and cheerful woman who had no bitterness in her heart. She made Birdie laugh when she started

asking was her lipstick looking well, and was her hair looking OK. No. Her lips were terrible. They were a fright. They
were like something out of a circus. And the few wisps of
hair on her bald head were like ragged wisps of sheep's wool
that hang off barbed-wire fences in the country.

But it was the quietness. There was something beautiful
about the quiet stillness of the hospice. And the low lights.
And the silent patients. Everyone waiting for the inevitable.

It was the end of the day. Birdie was alone and the
woman was dozing and waiting for her daughter to come
with chips. Gussie was sleeping and the place was lovely
and quiet and still, and the ward was full of curtains and
they all moved gently in the breeze. A draught that came
from the open door at the far end.

That's how it was. Lovely. And alone. And Gussie. And
the beautiful woman and the chips-daughter in the low
light. And everyone waiting. And Birdie alone.

Birdie was staring at the curtains and thinking how like
the rhythm of the sea they are. How like the waves of the
sea they are, billowing lightly in the blue breeze. And suddenly she saw him. He came from behind a curtain at the
far end of the ward. From an empty cubicle. There was no
one in there. Just an empty bed. She knew that.

And there was no bedside lamp glowing inside those
curtains. But the curtains moved. And opened. And she
saw him there, standing still and waiting and gazing right at
her. Neither hard nor soft. Neither angry nor kind. And she
was not afraid of him any more.

Wasn't she blessed to be alive? That's what Birdie was
thinking. Wasn't she blessed to be able to sit up in a chair,
as her comatose son struggled to breathe on one side of her,
and the beautiful daughter on the other side tried to land

drops of fizzy orange onto her beautiful mother's tongue.

And it was almost over. The end felt near. Close. And the night seemed pure.

That's all she could say to describe it. The night was pure. The universe suddenly seemed very simple. And the man behind the curtain was not going to harm her again.

She cried. It was a moment she could not explain to anyone. Not even the Vet.

From then on there was luminosity and stillness in the dying body, which even the priest remarked on when he'd visit.

'Isn't he very peaceful?' says the comical priest.

Yes, Father.

And the nurses got everyone to hold Gussie and rub his feet and his legs, and his arms and his chest, and his belly and the cheeks of his face. So much touching!

It should have ended there, but it didn't.

BIRDIE

I

BIRDIE DECIDED to go to Dublin. It was Tuesday. Or was it Wednesday? Well, it was the day before the snow.

It had been threatening all week, although the slanting November sun was blinding her eyes at the railway station. And the train pulled off under a pure blue sky.

She could hardly see out the window with the sun that day.

Cheerful is how Birdie described her condition. At the ticket office. Showing her free pass. Cheerful.

Because it was much more enjoyable to go off to Dublin for the day than to spend another endless vigil at the bedside with old Donoghue and that slapper Louise, in and out gawking at her as if she was the Mother of Jesus.

The bog rolled by and the sheep rolled by and two beautiful horses in a flat green field rolled by.

Cheerful. The trolley came with tea and coffee and a variety of raisin pastries. Birdie did a thorough examination but the boy's shirt was dirty, so she decided not to take anything, even though the little buns were all sealed up in plastic wrap. But you can't be too careful. She would buy jelly sweets in Dublin. She would have tea and buns in Arnotts. And she could be back home again on the evening train.

A mighty river stretched into the far distance as they approached Athlone. The shoreline came right up to the window of the train. The water was blue. She thought of Gussie. Blue for a boy.

He'd been lying in the same position now for over a month. His back and legs were sweaty and she had seen where cracks had appeared on the skin along the groin, and she had seen the nurses bathing him, and putting talcum powder all over his groin as if he were a child. He was a child. He was her child. But she hadn't powdered his body with talc for a very long time.

A big baby. That's what he was. Stuck in a big bed with cot-sides. And he was never going to be better. Of course not. He was going the other way. No wonder she didn't want to sit in the hospice staring at a big dumb baby. All his own fault for hitting a wall. Not looking where he was going.

In the old days she had chances. She could begin again. That was called being young, but she didn't know it then. When you could fail today and try harder the next morning. She could bake a special tart for him in the afternoon. She could let him help roll the pastry. Knead the flour. She could sit at the television with him for the children's programmes. She could put sweet rice in the oven for him. She could bring him into town on the back of her bicycle and get him comics and Spangles. But that was then. She could do nothing now. Not again. Not ever. He was as useless as a broken clock. And there was no point in the wide world sitting in a fucken hospice for the dying on a lovely day, punishing herself. What would she be doing that for?

And there was every reason to go to Dublin, on the train,

with her free pass, and enjoy the winter sunshine and look at the shops on O'Connell Street, and remember the time she bought the lovely material in Arnotts to make the cushion covers that still look so well on the drawing-room furniture.

2

A NUN CAME to Birdie's door the next morning. That was the first day of the snow. She was a small old lady with a shopping bag and puffed cheeks that drooped like a sad dog's, and her skin was purple from bad circulation.

Birdie never liked nuns. Why should she? But she let her in and made her tea, and they sat in the drawing room talking about the flecks of snow that were falling outside in the grey morning light.

The nun confided in her that she had spent two years attending psychiatrists and therapists, for depression, which had eaten her up since the incarceration of her local priest on charges of interfering with altar boys. Touching them. And making them use their mouths to touch him. Oh by Jesus, she had chapter and verse, this nun! She had suffered torments of unimaginable intensity, says she, in her lonely cell in the convent for a number of years, thinking about all those details. She was destroyed to think that the Church was rotten to the core. And humiliated every time she turned on a programme on the wireless or went into the shopping centre wearing her veil. Eventually it all became too much for her and she was taken away in the ambulance.

They gave her depression a name after a few weeks. It was a chemical imbalance of some sort, they told her, so she knew at least she wasn't responsible for that. They assured her that as long as she took her medication, she could live a normal life.

But it wasn't that easy to live a normal life, because the seven old ladies who made up the convent didn't want her miserable face and bleak emotions haunting the polished pine floor of their dining room any more. And so she was forced to find a small bedsit in the town and live whatever semblance of a nun's life she could, wandering around the town with her shopping bag, and praying in the back of the church, and delivering oranges and apples to the patients in the hospice.

While she was speaking, Birdie began to cry. It wasn't anything to do with the poor nun. Since the Vet had died, Birdie was used to nuns who would come to the door, sit down in the drawing room and tell her their life story before the kettle was boiled. But while she had been look-ing into the nun's eyes, a strange kind of panic crept up on her. An impossible sadness overwhelmed her. Maybe it was the dark sky, now full of snow, and snow falling in little flecks. Frantic. Like swarms of bees.

She interrupted the nun to explain that she must be leaving immediately for the hospice, because she had not seen her son since the day before yesterday. She rushed out into the garden, with no coat or shoes, and went down the avenue, into the snow, as if she was going to run all the way, and the nun still standing at the hall door in amazement, and the snow falling, first like bees swarming, and then, heavier, like tufts of cotton, floating to earth, and almost immediately weighing down the bushes.

Maybe it was lucky that the nun was there to go after her, though the nun didn't move. She was so stunned she just stood at the door. But then Birdie came back, for it had dawned on her that the nun was driving a little tin can of a car, and she could drive her into the hospice in twenty minutes. To see her son.

No bother at all, says the nun.

But in fact Birdie wasn't going to be seeing her son that day. No. Not ever again. For before the little tin can of a car came to a complete stop at the main entrance of the hospice, a staff nurse was already fussing around the vehicle, and opening the door and pushing a wheelchair into position in order to convey Birdie with the utmost speed down the quiet corridor that could well have been a convent in the previous century, and into the little enclosed cubicle where Gussie had choked on internal fluids thirty minutes earlier and passed away without struggle or distress, but alone, and with no witness.

He didn't look any different.

And – it must have been only seconds later – Hughie and Louise arrived, talking to each other about the snow that was falling, and they strolled into the cubicle and found a nurse sitting beside him and the sheet already pulled over his face. Birdie was in the family room talking to the priest about the funeral.

Was that yesterday? No. It was the day before. It had been snowing for two days. And the poor birds were starving. Pecking at the kitchen window. Especially the robin. Couldn't see in. But his little head was close up to the glass. Didn't have great eyesight, that wee robin. Not that Birdie's eyes were so good either. But she must leave a few crumbs out for them. Yes. That's what she should do. And she did it. Just like she should change out of her dressing gown and red slippers, and put on her black rags, and go to the funeral, at half-eleven. And she did that too. She did everything as everything should be done.

3

GUSSIE WAS BURIED on the last day of November, and his funeral passed off without much notice in the town. A small scattering of old friends gathered in the front pews around the grieving mother. The priest said something about life being a long walk, and that for some it's longer than others.

The coffin was bedecked with bouquets of flowers and the black hearse glided like a hovercraft through the main street of the town, with the required amount of dignity. Birdie sat in the back of a Mercedes that purred like a cat. Hughie Donoghue, old friend of the stricken mother, and Louise, erstwhile heart-throb of the deceased, either side of her on the black leather seats.

When nobody was watching them, they were all reasonably jolly. Birdie quizzed Louise on her plans. Louise said she was going back to Missouri. She missed her boyfriend, and he was helpless without her. Or was it Montana? It was definitely America.

Hughie stared out the window as Louise talked about her boyfriend, and he tried to study the slate roofs of the houses as if there was something interesting about them.

'So you'll not stay in Ireland?' says Birdie.

'No,' says Louise. 'There's no point.'

'No,' says Birdie.

'It wouldn't make sense. I have a job out there. Hanging

around Ireland hoping for a job to come up would be crazy.'

'Madness,' says Hughie. 'Pure madness. When you have the job over there.'

At the graveyard Hughie held the door open for Birdie as she struggled up out of the soft leather seat, and got a grip on her walking stick.

'You're fortunate, Mr Donoghue,' says she, 'to have your health.'

'Well, isn't that the truth,' says Hughie. Walking beside her all the time. Standing at the open grave beside her. Smoking a cigarette beside her when the prayers were over. His black tie flying across his shoulder in the wind, and a long streak of brown hair flapping into his eyes.

Louise and Birdie shook hands for the last time in Hayden's Hotel that afternoon, when the dinner was over. A good sturdy dinner of roast beef and potatoes, which Birdie had made available to all the mourners.

Louise hugged her. She kissed Hughie on the cheek. And then with her rucksack on her broad back, and her yellow anorak tucked up to her chin, and her long hair tucked in under a woollen hat with all the colours of the rainbow, she walked out into the snow and down the road towards the train station. They watched for a minute as she skidded a few times crossing the street.

'Will she be alright?' Birdie wondered.

'She'll be fine,' Hughie said.

Hughie lingered a little longer over his glass of Guinness and insisted Birdie take a brandy and port, which she did, though it never passed her lips. They talked about the dead. About dozens of people. Half the population of two cemeteries. People who died decades before. People who had stood in the same bar fifty years earlier. At Birdie's wedding. When Hughie had played 'The Dark-Haired Girl' to get things going. Her favourite polka.

Not that anyone would recognize the bar now. The way it was all changed. The door was in a different place. And the wooden counter had been gutted. With all the glass and fancy silver lampshades, Birdie said it looked more like a hairdressing salon.

He laughed. And for a split second anything might have happened. Maybe it was just that they both had the same sense of humour. Or that Birdie had none, and Hughie had enough for both of them.

And maybe that's why she confided in him on the day of her wedding, when her new husband was talking to his friend the priest, and Hughie was sitting in the corner of the lounge. His flute, idle on the tabletop beside his pint. Hughie relishing the blue smoke from the last cigarette in his packet.

'I'm worried,' she had told him then. 'I'm afraid to tell Alex. What will he think of me?'

Then in innocence she confessed her life to the flute player, simply because he was good-humoured, and she didn't know him, and she would probably never see him again.

'My strategy,' says Hughie, 'is always to confess everything before you get into bed. And anyway, in the heel of the reel, isn't he a Vet?'

And he winked.

That was a long time ago. But a terrible moment for Birdie, when a strange man would wink at her, on her wedding night.

'You've been a good friend to me,' says Birdie at the door of the hotel as they waited for her taxi, and Hughie shook her hand and called her Mrs Delaney. And then with a great warm smile on his long face, and his back as erect as a birch tree, he breathed her name for the first time. Birdie, he whispered. Birdie Waters. As if at last it might be acceptable to betray the Vet. Even if it was only in a whisper.

He stood in the snow a long time with his hand in the air. She watched him through the back window. He was the closest thing to Humphrey Bogart she had ever experienced. And he had a friend's ability to forget everything except her name. She waved through the back window until he was out of sight.

So there she goes. Up the long avenue and back to her own front door. The taxi crunching through the snow.

Will she be all right on her own? the taxi man wants to know. Of course she will. She pays him and waits to see the tail lights vanish at the bottom of the avenue. Waits until the muffle of the engine has died away in the distance.

She's alone at last.

And then she hears this noise. A flapping and a fluttering. And she goes round the side of the house and there's a bird spinning round in the snow. Like a boat out of control. He's trying to fly on one wing. The other limb trailing lifeless in the snow. He must have hit the window, she thinks. They're always doing that. Especially when there's a clear blue sky.

On closer inspection she discovers that it is her little robin. He is hardly able to see, and he doesn't notice her hand. Her two hands. So that now she has him firmly in her palms, and she goes carefully back round to the front of the house, and in the front door.

In the kitchen she gets a tea towel and lays it over him for a few minutes. He's trapped. Then she finds a sock in the laundry basket and cuts the top off with a scissors. It takes her a few attempts to get her hands back under the tea towel and then slip the bird into the sock. But finally she can expose him, and put him in a cardboard box by the range, with a saucer of water. The sock will hold the wing in place overnight. In the morning the bird will fly again.

Birdie has done this before. Many times. Though sometimes the bird is not so lucky. Sometimes all she finds on the doorstep are the dead feathers and bones that the cat left behind.

Is it their poor eyesight? she wonders. Or maybe it's the snow and the cold and the lack of drink that gets to their little brains and makes them do stupid things. Careless things. But she's glad she found him in time.

She closes the kitchen door and returns to the hall.

The robin is safe in the sock and she is safe in her house. Everything is in its place.

The little waterfont inside the hall door with the picture of Our Lady of Lourdes, and the bottle of holy water in the shape of Our Lady. Her seventeen coats under the stairs. Her shoes on the shelf and the shopping bags and umbrellas hanging from hooks on the wall under the stairs. The weather barometer in the hall where every morning she can still see the Vet tapping the glass with his knuckle.

She closes and locks all the doors. She locks the dining-room door, and the kitchen door. She bolts the front door. Three bolts. And ensures the new Chubb lock is secure. She ascends the stairs, which were first covered with green linoleum, and then with red carpet, and finally after the Vet died, in a grey wool, that is still fresh and clean and on which she has been ascending and descending on her bum for years.

She notices the name plate for the house, 'Ard Aoibheen', the Sweet Hill, that was wrought in Dublin, and fell off the front gate ten years after the Vet died, and which she left one day on the window ledge halfway up the stairs, not knowing what else to do with it. She notices the picture of the Vet with his high forehead and his cap and gown taken when he received his degree many years before she met him.

The pictures of Gussie on his First Holy Communion. Everything is in its place.

At the top of the landing four pairs of ancient spectacles rest on the dressing table. And the Child of Prague, which Gussie took the head off with a pillow when he was six.

And the bathroom with its soaps and jars and mugs of old toothbrushes, and a jumbo box of Radox. And Mickey Mouse and Donald Duck shampoo bottles from the time of Gussie's childhood. Her hot press with its sheets and blankets or what has not yet been stolen by invisible men who come still with regularity and deplete her supplies.

What does it all mean now?

The dressing table in her bedroom, with its powders and puffs, its towels and ointments. A faded picture of the Virgin Mary framed and hanging on the wall.

Her bedside lamp, the base of which she made one year at a wickerwork class run by the Widows' Association, after the Vet died and people said it would help her get over him.

Her wardrobe. Full of skirts, blouses, woollen frocks and beautiful linen suits for summer. Clothes she will never wear again.

A shelf with fifteen feathery little caps in blue and red, and white and black. A lifetime of little skullcaps.

An old orange clock that Gussie bought when he was going to the university. The brass bell they got in the early years of the marriage, which the Vet used if he was sick in bed, to call her attention from the kitchen. Envelopes she forgot to send to the priests. A bottle of Maalox for her stomach. A torch to see in the dark at night if she heard any unusual noises. The leather cover for a golf club, which she uses to hold small change.

Outside the snow continues.

Finally Birdie closes the bedroom door and turns the key, locking herself in, for security reasons.

She might wake during the night, but she has her bottle of water on the floor, and her radio on the pillow beside her. Another day is over. Another little triumph.